FREEZING IN DUVAL

THE TRILOGY

PART I

KEITH NESBITT

Copyright © 2023 Keith Nesbitt.

All rights reserved. No part of this book may be reproduced, stored, or transmitted by any means—whether auditory, graphic, mechanical, or electronic—without written permission of both publisher and author, except in the case of brief excerpts used in critical articles and reviews. Unauthorized reproduction of any part of this work is illegal and is punishable by law.

ISBN: 979-8-88640-830-0 (sc)
ISBN: 979-8-88640-831-7 (hc)
ISBN: 979-8-88640-832-4 (e)

Because of the dynamic nature of the Internet, any web addresses or links contained in this book may have changed since publication and may no longer be valid. The views expressed in this work are solely those of the author and do not necessarily reflect the views of the publisher, and the publisher hereby disclaims any responsibility for them.

One Galleria Blvd., Suite 1900, Metairie, LA 70001
1-888-421-2397

"Kevin, Kevin, boy get up!" was the sound of Kevin's mom as she tries to wake Kevin from his seizure. As Kevin start to come back to, Kevin's mother Hears the sound of the front door; where my food woman? Was all Kevin mother heard coming from the kitchen. Kevin's mother was in her thoughts, "I wish this man would just fall off the face of the earth, my mother fucking baby sick and he think..." and before she could finish her thought, she felt the whole side of her face was on fire. "Bitch, when I say something to you bitch that mean you answer me!!! Did you hear me, bitch? "please bae!! Please don't hit me my baby had another one of them seizures!" "Bitch, I don't care if that little bitch kick the mother fucking bucket. I better have hot food on that stove!! Do you hear me? said Big Kevin walking towards Claudette. Yes bae, but he's sick he might die!

While Claudette was trying to get her point across, Big Kevin punched her on the side of the head. "bitch, if you ever talk back to me again I'll kill you and that boy. I don't think he's mine any ways because none of my other kids have them damn things. I think it's the mother fucking milk man baby and if you ever say he's my son, I'll kill him first! Now get your dumb ass up and fix my fucking food and leave that damn retard right there, because I want to see him flap like a fish. As Claudette was getting off the hard cold floor she thought that when lil' Kevin gets old enough to make his own moves he was going to kill his father.

At the age of 9, lil' Kevin was moving around real good from his seizures. But Claudette always had trouble out of lil" Kevin from stealing car radios to stealing money from teachers. He stayed in DDC

(Duval Detention Center), that was lil' Kevin second home. The third was Mental Health Baker Act. See nobody knew or understood the things that went through lil' Kevin's head, all the mental and verbal abuse that lil' Kevin and his mother went through on a day to day basis was like hell. Like the week before lil' Kevin saw his father beat his mother almost into a coma, but the only thing that saved her was his hand broke. The only thing lil' Kevin could do was look because he couldn't even cry anymore. The next day lil' Kevin's mom yelled his name "Kevin, Kevin, boy while your ass sitting there looking in wonder land, you better have all these toys and shit picked up before that mad man come home cause I'm not trying to hear his mouth at all today.... but momma! My room clean! But ma can I ask you a question? Boy go ahead and don't be grown!! Ok ma, why we just won't move and leave daddy right here. Because we scared to in our own house that my check pay for! Boy, now I told your black ass not to be grown, now take your ass in that room and don't come out until you can be a child not a grown ass man!!! lil' Kevin walked off but in his mind his last day of abuse was soon to come. As time flew by lil' Kevin turned 11 years old and Saturdays was always crazy on Avenue B in the 80s with the Bull Dog Heavin and the Silver Star. These were the spots lil' Kevin loved to be around because all the old school niggas called him Freeze because lil' Kevin had one of the coldest hearts they seen on a jitt. "Hey Freeze, come over here and roll these dice for me" said old man Charlie. Shit, here I come old school. I know you going to buss down with me. "Jitt you already know money good in the hood, young blood, you better respect my gangsta lil' nigga" quoted big Charlie. Damn old school, I was just jiving with ya!" said Freeze. Well next time you know! now Charlie was a real gangsta. Charlie was one of the biggest hitmen on the streets in the 80's. Every dope boy, robber, or policeman feared Charlie. "Lil' Kevin grabbed the dice and shook it while talking. "Bitch I need a seven" then he threw the dice and just like that he called seven. "track and a dot pay the piper!" said lil' Kevin. "Lil' nigga I'm not bout to sit here and lose my money to no bad ass little boy!!!" yelled his opponent. "Old nigga I'm not no little boy you got me fucked" But before lil' Kevin could get his last word out, Charlie pulled out his two shot 38 and put a hot one in the middle of the guy head. "Dam Charlie you seen that?" Said lil' Kevin. That shit was crazy! Look and always remember this, never give anybody two chances because they lucky to have the first one.

When you get old enough you'll understand what I'm talking about said old man Charlie. From that day on, lil' Kevin never looked at life the same. He seen just how easy it was to be here one minute and the next you're gone. Lil' Kevin learned a real life lesson as he went deeper in the game. Lil' Kevin got far away from the world but as he walked his mind was taking him deeper into the foot steps of old man Charlie. From that day lil' Kevin was no longer lil' Kevin he was Freeze.

As Freeze walked home all kind of things drifted in his mind. But the only thing kept popping up were the words out of old man Charlie mouth and the dead body on the side walk. "hey young blood you got some spare coins on you, I haven't eaten in days" said the old man on the streets. "Man look this the first and last I'll ever give a grown ass man any money" said Freeze. Bless your lil' soul, God going to bless you young blood" said the old man. And old nigga I'll never be your young blood! Only one person call me that" then Freeze looked at him with a cold stare then turned around and finished his walk to Paris street. Momma where you at? "Here I go baby, I'm in the kitchen. As Freeze walked to the kitchen he could smell the fried chicken from the hallway frying in the deep frier. Ma that chicken smell good in here!! Why you in a good mode? Claudette just smiled. Well your father taking me out of town for the weekend!! And you going to your auntie house for the weekend and we'll be their to get you Sunday night!! said Claudette. Freeze couldn't do nothing but stand there with his head down. But ma I don't like going over there!! Their house be smelling like feet and it be nasty!! Boy I done told you to many times about being grown around here!! Now when you start paying some bills around here then your grown!!!! But... Before Claudette could get another word out Freeze pulled out a wad of twenty dollar bills and dropped it on the table... Claudette eye's light up... Boy I don't know where or who you done robbed for this cash!!! But when them white people come looking for your black ass!!! You going to jail!! And I'm not coming down their to sign you out either!!! So the best thing to do is take it back!!! NOW!!! And I mean right NOW!!!! said a upset Claudette. Freeze just looked at his mother for a minute. Ma listen!! I was on the block and a old kat name Mr Charlie asked me to help these people clean out his back yard!! And he paid us this! said Freeze. Claudette just shook her head. Boy!! God is my witness!! You pick the worst people in the world to be your friend's!!! said Claudette with hurt in her eye's. But momma he just looking out for me because he knew my sorry ass daddy don't do it!!! The look in Claudette eye's told many different tales. And it hurt it her that every word her son was saying was true. And she didn't know that life was going to be looking like this for them. Claudette just turned around and finished her meal because she knew this wasn't the life style she signed up for "Baby you ready? said Big Kevin. Naw not yet!! give me a few more minute's!!! I'm trying to get this boy stuff ready to go to Ruth house!! replied Claudette. Well ya'll hurry up!! I don't got all dam day!!! Now we got to stick to the strip!! As Big Kevin rushed around the side of the house. He had to make a pit stop. See Big Kevin had a secret life that nobody knew about but him. He had fell in love with a element. And it's name was free base.

As Big Kevin sat on his plastic cooler loading up his glass wife he reached in his pocket and grabbed his flame and beamed up to his own world. As Big Kevin zoned out he was wishing he could just trade his old family for his new one or they could just die. Was all Big Kevin could think about on his whole trip. But the the whole time Big Kevin sat on his cooler smoking Freeze just sat and watched his so called father suck a glass dick... 45 minutes later Big Kevin popped out of his daze to hear Claudette calling his name. Kevin!! Kevin!! Baby come on!!! And you talking about being late and on time!!! Now ... Before Claudette knew what hit her she was on the ground. Blood just rolled down Claudette face as she cried and talked. Baby please!!! I thought this was me and your weekend? I was just saying come on!! said a crying Claudette. Bitch!! Don't you ever in your life rush me!! And I'm not taking your mother fucking ass nowhere!!! Yelled Big Kevin. Freeze couldn't just sit around no more and just watch his mother get beat everyday. Nigga I'm sick of you hitting my mother fucking Before Freeze could draw back

Big Kevin was on top of him. Nigga now you think you grown now!! said Big Kevin. Now I'm going to give you that ass whipping you been looking for!!! The whole time Big Kevin talked he punched and kicked Freeze until he had a seizure. Claudette just looked and cried known that her son was near death. Kevin!!! Stop your going to kill him!! He's sorry!! Kevin please stop kill me!!! Lord please save my baby!!! cried Claudette. Bitch shut the fuck up!!! He think he grown!!! So I'm giving him what in the hell he need!!! said a mad Big Kevin. Before Kevin knew what hit him Claudette was punching and kicking him on the back. Get off my mother fucking baby!!! get off my mother fucking baby!! said a crying Claudette. Bitch get the fuck off my mother fucking back!!! I'm going to count to 10!! And if your not off my mother fucking back by then!!! I'm going to beat your ass just like I'm doing his!! Now 1,2,3 counted Big Kevin. And before Kevin hit four. Bitch get the fuck off my back!!! The force from the throw made Claudette head hit the side of the marble table. The way Claudette head hit the table made Big Kevin think she was dead. Oh shit baby I'm so sorry!!! Fuck this boy he could die!!! But I need you baby!!! Please wake up!! For daddy!!! As Big Kevin talked Claudette eye's was opening. When Big Kevin seen that he snapped. That's right bitch!!! You better not die on me you still owe me twenty more years!!! Now get your mother fucking ass up and clean that boy up and fix me something to eat before I whip your ass again. As Claudette struggled to get off the ground the only thing keep running in her mind was the conversation that her and Freeze had in the kitchen. And she knew if she didn't put a end to her and Big Kevin relationship soon that either he was going to kill her son or her son was going to kill him or worst.

Some time flew by. It seemed like Freeze was grown faster than the other children his age. When Freeze hit 13 years old he was looking like the average 18 year old. Everyday Freeze was on the block looking and learning. Old man Charlie had Freeze making sales on weed and stealing rims or braking into houses whatever it was Freeze was Mr Charlie man. Everyday some new game was getting pumped in Freeze vain's and everyday Freeze soaked ever drop of it. Hey young blood check this out for a minute!! I need you to make a run for me! said Old man Charlie. Freeze just turned around and walked over to Old man Charlie. What's up Old man Charlie? What's that you need me to do!!. said Freeze. Well I need you to run over to mike joe spot and pick up this chick for me!! Now listen!! This chick going to pay you for the ride!!! So take the keys and slide!!! And be careful out there!!! said Mr Charlie. As Freeze drove the only thing he could think of was how good it felt driving behind the wheel of a car that's not stolen. As Freeze drove people was waving and looking because nobody never seen anybody driving Mr Charlie car in the 50 years he been in the game now the streets knew who was Mr Charlie right hand man And the streets knew that it took a young nigga like Freeze to come alone and get molded for the crown of the streets.

But the only thing that was slowing Freeze up was the years he been on this earth. Before Freeze knew it he was in the front of mike joe spot. Man this bitch better be ready, thought Freeze. Beep Beep Freeze hit the horn and rolled a blunt and waited on the female Charlie sent him at.

As Freeze sat on the driver side of a smoke gray Delta 88 he seen one of the most finest black women he had ever seen in his short life span on this earth. As Freeze was in his thoughts he flinched when the passenger door opened. When the female sat down Freeze mouth was still open. Freeze didn't snap out his daze until he heard her talking. Hello!! I said my name is Mocha!!! What's yours? O shit my bad!! My name Freeze!! Now where you need to go sexy? Boy please!! I'm old enough to be your momma!! Or auntie or something!! Bitch you got me all the way fucked up!! I'm 18 years old I'm a grown ass man I take care of my mother fucking self!! So for now on you better respect me!!!! Or you can get the fuck out!! said a mad Freeze. The look in Mocha eye's made Freeze whole attitude change. Hold on now!! My bad little daddy!!! But I was just bullshitting with you!!! But I think what you just did was sexy ass fuck but you still to young!!! Because most niggas wouldn't even think about talking to me like that!! So this is a good start for a friendship!!! said Mocha. Well if this is a good start then when is we moving from in front of this place? said Freeze. But even if you were old enough you wouldn't want me I'm not really the girl that nobody won't! Because I sleep with men for money!! Or go out on dates with older men for money!! So that's the reason why I can't have a man in my life!! Because I have to many of them already!!! said Mocha. O ok I feel ya on that!! Now that's a rap!! So where do you need to get dropped off at? O shit my bad!!! You can drop me off on Lanes at the Hotel!! But! I have to make this pop first! Then I can pay you!!! Hold up! I thought you already had my money! There you go with these games! As Freeze talked Mocha just dropped her head. But Freeze I'm not on no games I got a pop to make and I got your money! Man fuck that fuck you pay me!! As the last words was coming out of Freeze mouth mocha was pulling out the money for the ride. See I knew you was with that fuck shit! But I'll holla at you later. As days turned into weeks and weeks into months Freeze birthday came fast. As Freeze laid in his bed dreaming a drift came threw his window that woke him up. When Freeze woke up he had a new out look on life, Everything was looking good for Freeze in the weed game, Because in the 80's everybody was on free base so they used the weed to come down so almost everybody came to freeze because he had the biggest dime bags and he had the best green. The only person Freeze got his work from was Charlie; And Charlie had the best in town. When Freeze turned 16 Charlie gave him ten pounds of mid with a ticket of 5,000. So Freeze was the man and nobody couldn't tell him no different. When Freeze got out his bed the first thing freeze did was brush his teeth and wash his face. Then Freeze walked in the front room and seen his mother sitting in her favorite chair reading the news paper. Hey ma what you got going on today? said Freeze while kissing Claudette on the cheek. Boy you know I don't leave out this house!! I don't have time for your basing ass daddy!!! See every since Claudette found out that Big Kevin was smoking free base she never looked at Big Kevin the same. And Claudette would always dream that she had the cash to leave. But the truth was, Freeze had went to Claudette on numerous occasions with the money to leave. But Claudette would never leave; She didn't know if it was the ass whippings or love, But Claudette knew it wasn't the love. But ma we can still ride to the movies or we can go grab a bite to eat!!! What's up? said Freeze knocking Claudette out of her day dream. Boy I don't know let me see what this nigga going to do! Then I'll let you know!!! Ok boy!!!! said a frustrated

Claudette. Well alright ma!! I already know you ain't going!! So I'm just bout to slide through the hood love ya ma!!! said Freeze as he walked out the front door. As Freeze walked out the front door the only thing Claudette could do was say a prayer for her baby because she knew the streets had her only child... When freeze hit the block everything was like a ghost town, So Freeze already knew where they was. Freeze walked to the new spot and walked in through the back door. Man what's up with all this shit up here? said freeze. I'm not trying to get screamed at about this mess ya'll made!! So move this shit off Charlie t.v!!! said Freeze. Jitt you act just like Charlie old ass!! said Frank. Now Frank was Charlie brother, Frank was a cool kat something like a pimp. See Frank had a fleet of females not whores, All uncle Frank female had jobs and they loved to take care of uncle Frank. Man I'm not trying to hear that shit Uncle Frank!! Because you know how your brother is about a nasty house!! said Freeze. Well I was just saying young blood!! said uncle frank still laughing at Freeze. Well tell pops I had to make a move!! I got to go check out this new chick!! said freeze. Alright be careful out there!! And do you got your fire? Said uncle frank. Old nigga I don't need a gun my name Freeze!!! I run these streets out here!! Old school!!! While the whole spot was laughing with freeze, Uncle Frank gave Freeze his final lesson. This is the last time I'll tell you this!! You should always have a piece on you!!! Because you'll rather get caught with it then dead without one!!! When Freeze heard that his mind went into overdrive. What type of tool you got!! Said Freeze. Well this is something you never knew about me this is the kind of work I specialize in!! Said uncle Frank. What can you handle? Well I'll rather have something I can take everywhere with me!! Said Freeze. Boy you smarter than you look!! said Uncle Frank with a smile. Ok I got a short barrel 357 you can have!! And a bet! If I ever catch you without it!! You pay me three hundred dollars!! said Uncle Frank. Ok!!! But if you ever ask me and I got it you pay me five hundred!! Said Freeze with a smile. That's a deal now let's shack on it so we can seal the deal!! Said uncle Frank. After freeze laughed him and uncle Frank shook hands then uncle Frank gave Freeze his first gun and from that day forward Freeze was never slipping... Freeze was walking in the parking lot of a Burger

King when a car pulled up on him. Boy I could've blown your head off!! said Freeze. But any way's!! I'm about to tell you just like I told that nigga tony!! Ya'll niggas posted up on my block like ya'll own it!! But I better not catch none of ya'll pumping anything on my street!! said the man in the car. Or I'll blow. The man in the car never seen freeze pulling out his gun, But when he did he only heard the sound of it Freeze stood in the middle of the parking lot hitting the back of the car. After every bullet was gone freeze snapped back to and noticed people walking out of stores looking at him with fear in there eye's. That's what made freeze tuck his gun and jump in the delta 88 and sped off into traffic. That was the first time freeze ever used a gun but it wouldn't be his last. It seemed like time was flying for Freeze it was 2 years since the incident and money was coming in from every way for freeze the streets belonged to freeze and he greeted it with open arms. But for every good thing theirs a bad. The thing that killed freeze the most was the fact that every time he left the house Big Kevin would beat his mother but freeze vowed that if he ever tried pulling a stunt like that while he was there he'll put a end to everything at that point. As freeze was in his zone he heard a voice. Hey bruh I need a OZ of that good pine you got!! said the voice. Man look for one!! Why you didn't beep me? said Freeze. Bruh I don't have your beeper number!! said the voice. So how in the fuck can you fix your mouth to ask me about anything illegal? Said freeze. Dam fam!! said the voice. Look main man!! You only have one choice and that's to leave!! So kick rocks while you still have that chance!! said freeze. As freeze sat there his mind was moving in overdrive the whole time. Man that nigga was the police!! said freeze. For now on I got to start watching every nigga or female that come around here!! Because I don't know who sent him at me but when I do they won't tell shit again on nobody!! said freeze with murder in his eye's. After freeze finished specking his mind to the block he walked to the Bulldog Heaven to let Charlie know what the play was. When Freeze walked inside the Bulldog Heaven he walked straight up to Charlie; Hey pops!! Let me tell you what just happened on the block! Some lame ass nigga walked up on me talking about he need a OZ of pine!! said freeze mad. But I never seen this nigga before a day of my life!!! Said freeze. So did you pop him off? What happened? said Charlie all ears. Hell mother fucking NAW!! I told that nigga the best thing he could do was get the fuck out of my face!! said freeze. Nine times out of ten that was the law!! So that mean you getting hot standing on that block all day and night!! So you need to find you a little spot that people can come and holla at you!! But still use your beeper! So you'll always know when somebody is coming!! So if somebody pop up then you know they the law!! said Charlie. Or the jack boys!! said freeze finishing off Charlie sentence. Plus only have in there what you plan on sale in for that day!! said Freeze. So you want me to find one now? said freeze with joy in his eye's. But where do you think I should get a house at pops? said freeze. Yeah I want you to get one around here because this is where all the money at!! But I want you to take a brake from the block for a little while until you cool off!! said Charlie. Ok pops I'll chill for a few weeks and start looking for a spot! But I'm also going to holla at Mr. James and try to work something out with him! But until then I'll be in the crib chilling! I'll call and check up on you until I get that spot!! said freeze. Alright be easy and get on that asap!! Because money need to be made!! And bills need to be paid!! said Charlie When Freeze heard that he walked out of the Bulldog Heaven and stood and thought about what Charlie just said and the only thing keep running through his mind was all the money that was about to come his way and he was about to get his own house. A week and a half had passed and everything had cooled down on the block. But freeze still had to wait until he found the new spot. But sitting in the house around his father was getting old real fast everyday it was something new that was being said. So everyday freeze tried to have somewhere to go so he wouldn't have to put up with Big Kevin bull shit. Freeze had already talked to Mr. James and the house was getting cleaned for him. So freeze knew he had that ready. But it wasn't moving the way he wanted it to. Thought Freeze. Three weeks had passed but if felt like a year. Freeze turned off the tv off and walked in his room to his closet to check his money. Because since he haven't been working money haven't been coming in so Freeze noticed every dollar that Big Kevin was stealing to feed his habit. As soon as Freeze opened his shoe box he noticed that a stack of money was gone. The only thing Freeze could do was shake his head and get dressed before he went off on his sperm donor. As freeze was leaving Big Kevin was walking out his room door. Looking clean as the state board of health counting Freeze money. Big Kevin never looked up to see Freeze standing there at the front door until it was to late. Dam nigga!! You just going to stand there and count my money in my face? said a mad freeze. Little nigga you better step the fuck back before I whip your mother fucking ass!! And take all your mother fucking money!! said Big Kevin. Freeze just stood there with murder in his eye's. Because he never thought a nigga would talk to him like that. But Big Kevin was the only person freeze had fear for so he just shook his head and turned around. Nigga you got that!! We good!! Have fun!! said Freeze. Walking out the door getting inside his delta 88 and pulled off down the street. When freeze pulled up on one of his homies he grew up with in Sherwood named Fresh.

See Fresh would always come chill with Freeze on the block and soak up game so every time freeze seen Fresh he would get fresh and lace him with as much game as he could. What's up lil bro? What the play is? said freeze. Man this shit been slow and hot!! So it ain't to much stuff going on my way I was about to call it a day and go home!! said Fresh. Shit I only made one hundred dollars out here all day!! said freeze. I'll take you to the house I need to clear my mind anyway!! said freeze. Hold on let me grab my stuff real quick!! said fresh. Nigga hurry up didn't you say it was hot out here? Nigga come on!! said freeze. As fresh was grabbing his work Freeze just looked at the block and knew it was his for the taking. As Freeze and fresh rode they talked about everything that was going on in there life. Man bro my momma been tripping on me about school and I'm sick of it!! And I'm sick of her mouth!! said fresh. But I got some money put up!! And I want to invest in something big!! Ya feel me bruh? said fresh amped up. Little nigga you know I understand!! So get to the point!! said Freeze. What you talking about getting? Shit I got about five grand put up and that's what I want to put in the pot!! said fresh. Either I'm going to bust or blow!! So what's the play? said fresh. Well you know I keep the best!! So I got to put a little tax on the ticket!! So I'll give you each pound for nine hundred a piece!!

So that's 4 ½ pounds!! said freeze. But I'll put the other half with it so you'll have five pounds!! said freeze. So the next time have everything lined up straight cause you already know I keep the best green around this bitch!! said freeze. So what's going on with you and your family? said fresh. Boy let me tell you about this fuck ass nigga!! said freeze. Who your daddy? said fresh. Yeah!! That fuck nigga!! said freeze. This nigga been stealing my money! Dam what you going to do about it? said fresh. Shit I just found out today! Something told me to go in the room and count my cash, When I did it was 1,000 dollars short!! said freeze. Then this nigga was walking out his room, Clean ass fuck counting my cash!! Now this the crazy shit he call his self checking me about my cash!! This nigga really must of lost his rabbit ass mind g-shit lil bruh!! said freeze. Dam bruh so what you going to do about that!! said fresh That nigga stealing now!! That's fucked up Big Bruh!! said fresh with anger in his voice. On some real nigga shit I'm sick of that nigga. He got one more time to try me and I'm going to flat line his bitch ass!! said a mad freeze. Bruh that's your daddy spare him!! On my face!! said fresh known Freeze was serious. That shit written in blood already!! So let's end this before it go somewhere else!! said a mad Freeze. Well I feel ya bruh!! But come on in the house so I can grab this cash for ya!! said fresh getting out the car. But on some real nigga shit bro!! I said what I said out of love because I don't want to see nothing happen to you that's all!! said fresh. I just don't want nothing to play you off the streets that's all bro!! I feel ya bruh but lets come on before your momma come home!! said Freeze. Because I'm not trying to hear her mouth! As they walked through the house fresh kept talking about different stuff he had planned. Bruh on some real nigga shit I'm going to blow! I'm going to flood the streets watch what I'm telling you!! said fresh. And I'm sale in all quarters! For 30 dollars a piece! How that sound? said fresh. Shit that sound good you'll make around 1,680 a pound! That's a good start you just got to stay focused on your grind that's all!! As they sat in the room doing numbers fresh heard the front door open. Dam man now I got to hear this shit!! said fresh. I can't wait until I get old enough to get my own place!! said fresh. But come on before she come back here and count your cash first!! said fresh. As Freeze started counting his money all hell had broke lose. Boy I have told you to many times about having people in my shit!! You don't pay no bills around here or your not in school!! So you need to make up your mind because I'm about to put your grown ass in foster care!! Because my house is not big enough for a grown woman and a broke ass grown man!! said fresh mother. Now this is my last time telling you why you out there petty hustling making yourself hot! You need to get your mind right! And you and your friend get the fuck out of my house!! said fresh mother. And by the way how you been doing Kevin? said fresh mother. O I been good Miss Mills!! said freeze getting up. I'm about to leave now Miss Mills!! said freeze again walking out the door with a bag of money.

Outside looked like some shit was about to go down. Freeze and Fresh sealed the deal and plan for the drop to be the next day. Time flew as Freeze talked to Fresh. Freeze needed to see Fresh because every time he sees Fresh he has something new going on and it's a come up that he always be talking about. Freeze pulled up in the driveway and seen something wasn't looking right inside the house so he took his time and walked around the house to check the scene.

When he made it to the front door and seen a scene that would never leave his mind for the rest of his life. He seen blood everywhere in the living room, so as Freeze rushed to find his mother he seen his dad beating his mom. She was inches from her death when he snapped and walked up on his father, the only man that he ever feared and pulled the trigger of the 357 and just stood there. When Claudette heard the blast from the gun and seen all of big Kevin's brains on the wall, she jumped up and grabbed the gun from Freeze. "Baby, baby! Look I'm so sorry for everything I put you through in life I should have listened to you that day in the kitchen but love had me blind; I can't let you go down for this at all get your stuff and leave, hurry up!"

As Freeze momma was talking, he snapped back to and ran into his room grabbed his money and a few outfits and left. The whole time Freeze packed Claudette was building enough courage to pull the trigger on herself. As Freeze walked out the house Claudette found the courage to pull the trigger.

After the suicide of his mother and the murder of big Kevin, Freeze put his all in his hustle. Mr. James gave Freeze the house in the hood and Freeze blew up asap. He had the whole North, East and West on lock down. Everybody in the streets respected Freeze and always paid him. Charlie molded Freeze and he had everything in heart that Charlie showed him. After he killed his father, Freeze never gave anyone more than one chance and one chance only because he knew if he didn't the streets will swallow him whole. He put his all in the game not head first, but just dived in with no understanding at all about anybody's life in or out the game. It was a Tuesday, three days before Freeze's birthday. So he was making plans for for his day it was going to start with a cook out then the hood was going to the silver star that's in the hood so Freeze stepped out the trap to see one of his homies. "Nigga what you got going on here, you're a long way from home" I wasn't looking to see you walk out the house what it do I need to rapp a taste with you" said Phil. Go ahead, what the play is? Asked Freeze. What it's sour or what?" Bruh you know I'm not the type of nigga that run with shit but I was on the south side shopping with a nigga named Killer when one of Killer boys walked in with a girl name mocha. Now this was a fine ass bitch, so anyway the bitch pulled the lil" nigga to the side and they started talking and I can only hear the girl saying "No, but before anybody else say anything. Killing you and taking all your work". Hold the fuck on, so you telling me this bitch Mocha and a nigga that you don't know his name!!! said Freeze. "I never said I didn't know his name" said Phil.

The lil' nigga name is Fresh that was with her, but the lil" nigga Fresh said that you'll trust him enough to let him in then that's when the other two niggaz suppose to run in and kill you" said Phil. The only thing I have to say is "be careful bruh". Bruh on some real nigga shit I'm going to just chill and close down for a little minute to let the heat die down. "well I was just letting you know what was going down! I got one question for you bra... What's up! Well I been thinking about everything you told me and I see a lot of loop wholes in your shit because first of all these niggas that you getting work from just letting you listen in on them talking about killing me!! said Freeze. I'm not no any type nigga!! said Freeze getting madder by the minutes. So you need to come out and let me know what part you playing in this fuck shit!! said Freeze pulling out his 357. Because this shit just got real!! said Freeze pointing the gun at Phil head. Please Freeze!! said Phil with fear in his voice and eye's. The whole time Phil was begging for his life he never seen the person walking up behind him!! Freeze you good bruh? said Blaze one of Freeze right hand men. Who this fuck nigga is? Yo Blaze I'm happy you came up!! Take this nigga in the house!! He got some info I need!! said Freeze. As Blaze took Phil in the house Freeze went in the bathroom and lined every inch of the floor with trash bags and plastic. Once Freeze finished his job Blaze pulled a screaming Phil to the hallway while Freeze helped Blaze put Phil body in the bath tube. Once Phil was in the tube Freeze went to work!! Now I'm going to ask you this one more time!! Then I'm going to let Blaze do his thing with ya!! said Freeze with a smile on his face. Now how you want it? asked freeze. Freeze!! Freeze!! Please I'll tell you everything you want to know just don't kill me PLEASE!!!! said a crying Phil. Look nigga!! said Freeze with murder in his eye's. Now this is how I want it!! Nigga I want the whole lay out from the time you woke up until the time you came to me with this fuck shit!! said Freeze. And if for any reason I feel like your lying!! I'm going to kill you at that point!! Now do we have a understanding? said Freeze. Yes!! Mr Freeze!! Now this is how it went! Me and fresh always been home boys! From the first time we grabbed some work from you it's been a set up!! said Phil still crying to Freeze! But we never had a good way to do it so we figured we'll have to come at you a different way!! So that's when Fresh started talking to a female named Mocha!! said Phil thinking what he was saying was saving his life. Fuck nigga get to the point before I bust your head open!! said a mad Freeze when he heard Mocha name. Alright Please!! Don't kill me Freeze!! cried Phil. They told me to come over here and see if this was your trap house!! So that's why I came!! But when I seen you my heart wouldn't let me do it!! Please believe me Freeze!! said a begging Phil. I put that on my mother life!! So you telling me you didn't know that the person they was talking about was me? said Freeze getting madder and madder the more Phil talked. Fuck nigga you about to die if you don't tell me where these mother fuckers at!! And I'm talking about asap!! said

Freeze moving closer to Phil. It's 4215 Coco St off of Acme on the South side!! cried Phil thinking his life was safe. When Phil seen the look in Freeze eye's he started to beg more for his life. Please don't kill me!! I'm just trying to eat that's all Kev!! cried Phil looking Freeze dead in the eye's. Fuck boy you know you dead off of what you did!! said Freeze. Now!! If you would tell on your right hand! I know you'll tell them boy's on me!! said Freeze with a smile on his face. So I'll holla at you pimp!! When Freeze said that Blaze walked up on Phil and stabbed him with a kitchen knife until all the movement was gone out of Phil body. When Freeze seen all the life leave out of Phil body he turned around to leave but turned back to holla at Blaze, Hey bruh look into that for me!! I need that handled by friday!! said Freeze walking out the bathroom door. I got you bruh was the last thing Freeze heard before he walked out the house. After the incident with Phil Blaze went straight to work watching the house on on the south side. A day and a half had passed before Blaze seen who he came to see; Around 9 o'clock that night Blaze seen a car pull up in the driveway and a female and a nigga got out and from what Blaze knew it was Fresh and Mocha. So Blaze sat outside and waited to see how long they was going to chill. Blaze sat inside his car and waited until he seen the sun pecking from over the tree's. Then he seen the front door open and Fresh walk out with a bag and jumped in his car and pulled off. When Blaze seen that he grabbed his phone and called Freeze. Before Freeze could say hello Blaze was talking. Yeah this me! I just seen that fuck nigga Fresh pull off!! But that Bitch Mocha still inside the house!! What you want me to do about that? said Blaze. Shit you already know what I want you to do to that shit!! said Freeze out of his sleep. And make sure that Bitch pay the piper! I got ya bruh!! said Blaze getting ready to make his move. Once Blaze hung up his phone he walked up on the house and looked through every window until he seen Mocha walking around the house naked listen to music that's when Blaze slide in and made his move... Inside the house Mocha was getting ready to take a bath so she rolled a joint and turned head under her Keith Sweat on her tape player and walked around the house. As Mocha walked she never noticed the shadow behind her until it was to late... Mocha was in the bathroom checking her water when Blaze walked up behind Mocha grabbed her around the neck and stuck her head up under the water until there was no more movement in Mocha body. When Blaze seen there was no more movement his mind went straight to clean mode. As Blaze was cleaning the crime scene he heard the front door open and Fresh walk in. So Blaze mind snapped back into beast mode and slide down the hallway into a closet and pulled out his 38 special and watched everything through the cracks in the door. When Fresh walked in he snapped. Dam didn't I tell your ass to lock the Mother fucking door!! Now supposed somebody just walked in this mother fucker and blow your mother fucking head off don't call... Before Fresh could finish his sentence Blaze jumped out the closet and hit him three times in the chest. Once Fresh fell Blaze walked up and hit Fresh three more times in the face to show the world what happen when you cross Freeze and Blaze. After Blaze cleaned everything he touched he grabbed the bag of money and work and walked back to his car and headed to holla at Freeze. Freeze was sitting in Charlie kitchen watching him brake down bricks into eighth's; While uncle Frank was cooking up 28 in the 8. Freeze just sat there and got his lesson. When Charlie finished braking down he counted and seen that Frank was on his tenth cookie that's when Charlie laid everything on the line for Freeze. Now son!! said Charlie looking at Freeze. Don't you think it's time for you to up grade in money? said Charlie with a slight smile on his face. Now!! I'm not saying weed money ain't good money!! But when you move your game to this white girl!! said Charlie holding up a brick so Freeze could see it. Then you'll see way more money then you did in the weed game SON!! I'll Show you everything you need to know about this white bitch!!! I feel ya pop's!! But I don't know about that line of work G-Shit!! said Freeze looking confused. Cause I got good money coming in on the green so I just don't see myself switching over right now that's all pop's!! said Freeze looking down thinking he just broke his father heart. Well whenever your ready I get this shit by the truck loads!! said Charlie still looking at Freeze. So let me know when your ready like I said!! I will Pop's!! It might be real soon!! said freeze standing up to walk over to Charlie and Uncle Frank. But what's the ticket on this stuff? said Freeze just to have that much in his head for future purposes. Well!! said Charlie ready to give Freeze his lesson. For the brick!! It's 25 to 26 thousand!! But on these here eighth's!! They going to run you about 26.5 or 27 hundred. And that's 4 and a half ounce's!! And that Shit move like a speeding train!! said Charlie getting hype as he talked. Now when you ready to learn how to cook!! Let me know or your Uncle here know!! Ok? said Charlie. Yes Sir!! said Freeze sitting down from the lesson. But before I forget here's this thing for your birthday!! And Charlie pulled out a black bag and gave it to Freeze!! Happy Birthday son!! said Charlie. Freeze looked at the bag and knew it was money so he dumped it on the table and started counting. Thank you Pops!! said Freeze moving around the money. How much this is Pops? It's about 15 thousand so tomorrow do your thing!! said Charlie with a grin on his face. Come on Frank let's slide so this boy can do his thing!! said Charlie as him and Uncle Frank grabbed there bags and walked out the spot. After about a hour Freeze sat in the trap thinking about what was going down for tonight. So Freeze started to get ready; He had already hit up J J Riggings in the Jacksonville Landing in Downtown Duval. Freeze had grabbed three New River outfits and three pair of Dice's to go with his outfits. Freeze walked in the bathroom to clean his self up when he heard Blaze calling his name. So Freeze finished up and walked in the kitchen dapping Blaze up and sat down while Blaze gave him the run down. Man bruh that Shit was crazy ass Fuck!! said Blaze with a black bag on the table. These mother fuckers left the front door open!! said Blaze putting out money pulling them into different stacks. So after I knocked off Mocha that fuck nigga came in and I put it him raw G-Shit!! said Blaze. And they had this money and work!! It's about 50 thousand in there so here's your 25 thousand and I'm going to keep the work!! said Blaze passing Freeze his cut of the money. So what that fuck nigga said before he died? I didn't give that Nigga a chance to speak his time was up!! said Blaze. Freeze just laughed and looked at Blaze; That's what's up I'm about to get clean for tonight! said Freeze. I'll be ready around 6 o'clock! said Freeze walking towards the back room of the house. That's what's up was all Freeze heard before the door closed... 6 o'clock came fast and the parking lot was full of people and the D.J had everybody vibe in to the latest toon's, While

Nigga's and female's was fixing drinks and smoked joint's that freeze already had ready for his guess. Freeze just walked around until he made it to his table and sat down then about 30 minute's later Freeze seen Blaze walking up on the table. Happy Birthday my nigga!! said a smiling Blaze. Nigga I know you feel old! Because you look like you about 21 or something!! said Blaze with a smile on his face. Nigga you got me fucked all the way up!! said a smiling Freeze. Nigga I'm only 17 years old!! But one thing about it is!! I got more money then any nigga my age or older so I'm living Bruh!! said Freeze giving Blaze a hand shake. But look at all these mother fuckers out here!! That don't even fuck with us!! said Freeze But these fuck niggas only out because shit free! And these hoe's trying to catch a lick!! This shit crazy but it's my day so I'm about to have some fun!! O yeah bruh before I forget!! said Blaze pulling a bag out of his pocket. I checked with one of my white boy's and he gave me these pill's with face's on them! He say they X- pills or something!! He said they going to make us roll!! said Blaze looking at Freeze. Nigga these mother fuckers look like flint stone pills!! said Freeze looking at the pills. I'm not popping one of them you crazy boy!! said Freeze laughing. Dam bruh!! You can't pop one of these with me for your birthday? said Blaze. I thought I was your right hand man? I'll never do anything to hurt you!! said Blaze with a serious look on his face. You know what bruh!! You dead ass right give me one of them mother fuckers!! said Freeze while he grabbed his pill from Blaze hand. Now my home boy told me these pills will have you doing whatever's on your mind before you take it!! So if you have anything crazy on your mind don't take it!! said Blaze. Nigga I'm good I'm not slow!! You shouldn't never take one because your mind stay on some cut throat shit!! said Freeze with a smile on his face. Not today bruh it's your birthday!! Now let's take the pill!! said Freeze. As Freeze and Blaze sat on the back of Blaze truck. Freeze just started to sweat out of nowhere. First Freeze took off his hat and jumped off the back of the truck. Then out of nowhere he started to talk. Bruh!! Pop's put a bug in my ear the other day! Talking about getting money on a real nigga level!! What do you know about coke? said Freeze still sweating and gritting his teeth from the pill. Shit I know that shit will put some real coin's in our pocket's!! And have us hot ass fuck too!! said Blaze moving to the music. Bruh we won't be on no little boy shit!! We'll be selling in eighth's or better!! Making some real money on some G-Shit!! So what's up bruh? What you want to do!! said Freeze with a look of a monster. Shit bruh you already know I'm down with whatever go's down with the family!! So when we switching bruh? said Blaze with greed in his eye's. Well first we have to find somebody we can put in the weed spot!! Then we need another spot for the coke!! said Freeze with dollar sign's in his eye's. Well that's some shit there!! Because we don't really fuck with to many people!! So that's something you'll have to figure out on your own!! said Blaze with a lost look in his eye's. Shit I got a better plan!! said Freeze. How about I work a spot and you work a spot!! And we do everything like we do the weed!! Everybody call no walk up's!! said Freeze ready to get money. So what's up with the customer's? We need to start meeting people for the coke!! said Blaze. Shit that's the easy part there bruh!! Because everybody that get green from us know somebody that know somebody!! So that's how we'll move the word around!! said Freeze ready to get money. So you saying we'll have random people calling our phone for coke? said Blaze. Nigga you slow ass hell!! said Freeze and busted out laughing. The only way a nigga get served is if he come with who told him!! said Freeze. But I think it'll work bruh!! said Blaze. Shit bruh I know it's going to work it have no choice!! said Freeze with sweat running down his face. But bruh it's hot ass fuck out here and the sun done went down so I'm about to head to the spot and take a shower and get dressed for tonight!! What you about to do? said Freeze. Shit! Let's roll! I got my stuff in the truck!! said Blaze opening up the truck door for Freeze. When Blaze pulled up to the spot he pulled his 38 from out the arm rest and Freeze grabbed his 357 from off his lap and they walked around the house to make sure everything was safe once they met up at the back door they walked in and got there self together for tonight. When Freeze got out the shower Blaze was already dress and was on the sofa smoking a joint when Freeze hit the corner. Dam bruh I almost kicked the door in!! said Blaze laughing. Nigga these pills had that shower feeling so good I almost went to sleep in that bitch!! said Freeze laughing and still drying off walking to the room. When Freeze walked out the room he was fresh to death!! So where your boy get these pills from bruh? said Freeze braking down some weed for tonight. I don't know bruh I know his daddy is a hippie on some save the world type shit so I don't know if he can get them again or not! But I'll see what the play is for us bruh!! said Blaze getting so they can leave. I feel ya on that bruh!! Cause that shower did fell good as hell!! said Freeze. But I got us some rooms on the beach and some bitches for later!! So I'll drive tonight!! said Freeze. So when we go to the club we'll just chill for a few hours then we'll leave before anybody start to leave!! That's what's up!! So come on before it get to late!! said Blaze. When Freeze and Blaze pulled up inside the parking lot of the club. It was packed with nowhere to park but by Freeze an Blaze being who they were. They had parking already ready for them in the front of the club. Shit that's what's up here bruh let's gone in the inside and see what's going on in this bitch. When they walked in everybody was looking and pointing at them so Freeze and Blaze walked over to there table and popped there bottles and made there rounds through the club. As Freeze and Blaze was walking Freeze felt somebody touch his arm that made him turn around. Hey baby sorry for stopping your movement!! But ya'll the cleanest niggas I've seen since my son on Easter Sunday!! Thank you baby girl!! We just felt like over doing it tonight that's all little momma!! said Freeze while pulling out a napkin. Here little momma take this napkin and put it to use!! said Freeze moving through the crowd. When Freeze turned around he didn't see Blaze so he keep on walking talking to people that he knew from the block and some people that was just showing love. When Freeze stopped walking he seen Blaze walking with a bottle of 1738 and a bucket of ice and two cups but the same female that stopped Freeze walked back pass him and slide him the same napkin he gave her and walked off before Blaze could walk up. Dam bruh who that little Bitch was? said Blaze pouring him and Freeze a drink. She was fine ass hell but her friend was ugly ass fuck!! said Blaze laughing out loud. Shit I don't know but it say baby face on the napkin!! But if she can't put her real name on this bitch then she really ain't trying to fuck with me so lets just do a walk through and see who all came out to support me on my day!! said Freeze while Blaze grabbed the bottle and led the way. As Blaze led the way through the club they seen all the local dope boys and the local jack boys everybody came out to show love to a real nigga. As Freeze and Blaze walked they noticed a nigga watching them so they slowed up and let the person catch up. But before Freeze could say anything Blaze already had his 38 pointed in the nigga chest. Fuck nigga what's up with you? said Blaze with his gun in the dude chest. You been watching us since we started walking!! what's up with that!! said Blaze pulling his hammer back on his 38. Freeze you already know why I'm here tonight!! said Killer with murder in his eye's. But I came unarmed!! And with no back up! I came so we could rap a taste!! said Killer. Look Killer I should blow your mother fucking spine out your back for even much walking up on me like that!! We don't have shit to talk about!! Your nigga was plotting to rob and kill me so he got what he was looking for!! So get the fuck out my face G-Shit!! said Freeze with murder in his eye's. And better yet!! The next time you see me you better have your fire!! If that's how you feel I'll be seeing you real soon!! said Killer and turned around to walk out the club but he never seen all the other eye's on him as he walked out the door. That nigga really got some balls walking up on a nigga why we chilling!! said Blaze. But while Blaze was talking some young nigga's walked up on Freeze with murder in there eye's. Bruh you want us to handle that for ya'll? said one of the little nigga's. Look!! I got one order!! said Freeze. Ya'll make sure ya'll do it out the hood!! And hurry up before he get away!! said Freeze with murder in his eye's. We got it bruh!! said one of the young Nigga's before they ran out the club through the back door. Come on bruh let's finish the rest of our night!! said Blaze turning around to leave. When Freeze little home boy's pulled out of the club they seen Killer leaving out the same way they was so they strapped up and followed him into a Hess gas station. When Killer pulled up to the gas pump the Buick Skylark pulled up the the pay phone and watched Killer every move... Freeze and Blaze pulled inside the Hilton and drove straight to the velet gave them there room number's and walked to the elevator. When Freeze and Blaze stepped off the elevator the felt like they was home sweet home until they walked in there rooms;

When they stepped in it was drugs of every kind and every female was walking around nude. When Blaze seen that he couldn't whole back. Now bruh!! I know it's your birthday! But I'm about to go crazy with all these bad ass slut buckets in this bitch!! said Blaze as he was taking everything off but his shoe's and sock's. Freeze was in the same motion when the door from the joining room came open. When they ran in they had no chance. The first person Freeze hit in the neck, While the second person tried to get low but the bullet hit him in the arm that he was holding his gun in. Before the first body hit the ground Blaze had his 38 in his hand's in enough time to hit the third person four time's in the body. As Freeze made sure everybody was dead Blaze walked over to his cloth's and started putting them on. As soon as Blaze went to put his pant's on he never seen the female grab a steak knife from under the pillow and run behind Blaze and stabbed him in the back with the knife. When Freeze heard the female voice he turned around to see a female about to kill his right hand man that's when Freeze put three bullet's in her back then walked up on her and put the other three in the back of her head. That's when Freeze heard like some people gagging in the other room. When he walked in he seen diamond and dime tied up on the side of the bed on the floor. The first person Freeze untied was Dime. As soon as the gag was off her face she went to talking; Baby I swear we had nothing to do with this!! That fuck ass Bitch Money set all this up!! said Dime in fear of her life. We had nothing to do with none of this creep ass Shit!! I swear to the Almighty God we didn't!! said Dime crying more. So who in the fuck these Nigga's is? said Freeze getting ready to knock her off. "Ok"!! That one right there with the half a head!! That's Money baby daddy!! And he got a brother name Killer that be on the south side!!! So you mean to tell me this bitch or this nigga never asked ya'll did ya'll want in on this? said Freeze not believing her story at all. I swear to God on my kids that I never thought of doing no shit like this to you!! said Dime scared for her life now because she knew Freeze wasn't buying her story at all. Because you came to us with this and put it together!! Please don't kill us!! cried Dime. You can stop all that crying!! Because you and this Bitch was the only people knew we was going to be in the Starr tonight!!

But on the good side both of ya'll time is almost up!! said Freeze lifting his arm but before he could shoot he seen Dime body go limp so Freeze turned around and shot Diamond in her face then ran over to Blaze. Dam Nigga I thought you was dead!! I was about to kill that bitch I just needed that info I just got off her ass!! said Freeze looking at his ace laying in his own blood. Man this bitch hit me in my shoulder!! I need to hit that hospital in Kingston Ga!! said Blaze getting up off the ground. When Freeze seen Blaze up on his feet. He did his round's around both room's and grabbed everything that they had when they walked in and left out through the fire exit door headed for the hospital... When Killer parked his car at the pump he heard his phone but before Killer answered he paid for the gas and walked to pump it but his phone was still ringing off the hook. When Killer answered the only thing he could hear was the voice of his baby momma. Dam Nigga!! It's almost 5 in the morning and your black ass still outside? said the voice on the other end. Man fuck that shit you talking right now!! said a mad Killer. Them fuck nigga's killed my brother the other day!! So them nigga's got to die right along with him!! said a even madder Killer. Baby I understand that but I'm the one that be getting the work from him! So if his people find out that you kill him or trying to kill him! They going to come after me and my children!! Not you!! said a crying voice. Look Bitch! I need you to holla at them nigga's later this afternoon and get some work!! And I mean you better do what I'm telling you to do!! Do you hear me talking to you Bitch!! said a mad Killer. I hear you but I only have one last thing to say to you!! said the crying voice. After this last lick! I'm done with you and this life style!! said the crying voice before she hung up. Hello!! hello!! I know dam well this bitch didn't hang up that phone in my face! said a mad Killer. But instead of Killer calling her back he just tried to pump his gas but the pump wasn't on. So Killer walked back in the store and got in line. Outside Freeze little goon's was trying to get everything ready when they seen Killer walk out the store and walk back over to his car and got on the phone. Now look!! We need this hit!! After we do this Freeze going to look out for us!! Now we going to hit that nigga when he start pumping his gas so we won't even have to get out the car at all!! We'll make it look like a drive bye!! said the driver. But as the driver was talking Killer was walking back in the store. Nigga why you thinking you the Boss!! The nigga just walked back inside!! said the passenger. Now since we know who the Boss is!! This how we going to do this!! When he walk out the store and start pumping his gas we going to do a walk up!! said the passenger. Now shut the fuck up and get ready. Inside the store Killer got the clerk straight and grabbed some Newport 100's and and tried to call Dime but every time Killer called he got no answer so Killer looked around and seen a police sitting on the other side of the store so he walked out to his car and started pumping his gas. As Killer was pumping he never saw the two young killers slow walking behind him until it was to late. The first bullet missed Killer head by inch's. That made Killer reach for his gun. When the second young killer seen that he gave Killer every bullet he had in his gun, Why the other killer walked up on him and shot him two more times in the head. On the other side of the building the police officer was calling back up. Come in!! Come in!! said a scared officer. Shot's fired!! I repeat!! Shot's fired!! At the corner of Atlantic and Beach!! Once the officer called back up he made his move around the building and what he seen made him sick to his stomach. He seen a man just standing over another man shooting him to death. When the officer gained his focus his two suspect's was running back to a Brown Buick Skylark. When the officer seen that he ran to his car and made pursuit on his suspect's. Calling all car's!! Be on the look out for a stolen Brown Buick Skylark with two black young male's look around the age of 18 to 21 I'm in pursuit... said the officer before he hit his light's. Inside the car the young killers was happy about the hit. The first thing the passenger did was grab the half a jay that was in the ash tray. That's what I'm talking about there bruh! We need to go to the hood and holla at Freeze!! said the driver happy about the hit. Nigga let's get the fuck from. Before he could get the last word out they seen the light's. Dam where that mother fucker came from? said the driver scared to death. Shit I don't know but we need to come up with something fast and I mean fast!! But I can tell you one thing I'm not going to jail for murder!! said the passenger reloading his gun. Nigga is you crazy!! I'm not killing no police officer!! You can but I'm not; I'm about to pull over. With them last words the passenger looked over at his best friend and blew his brain out on the driver side window. When the car jerked the passenger grabbed the wheel and slide on top of his dead friend to drive the car. After a minute he snapped back to and realized he had killed his best friend since grade school. And the first person his mother was going to say was his name. 15 minutes later he felt the car get hit and do a 360 and hit a pole. But the impact from the pole didn't stop the young killer from finishing his job. Freeze!! Freeze!! Put your hand's up where I can see them!! said the voice of the police officer's. The sound of the horn made the little killer wake up from his daze in straight attack mode. The young killer door was already open from the impact, So he just went into action. Fuck all you pussy ass crackers!! said the young gun man as he jumped out the car with his gun blazing. As he tried to move to a safe spot to shot he got hit four times. The first one hit him in the upper torso. While two hit him in the leg's and the last one hit him in the face. When the smoke cleared the gun man was face down in the street and the police was giving each other high five's and pat's on the back. Two month's after the death of Freeze two assassin's and the attempt on his and Blaze life they sat in the house talking to Charlie about the switch. Look son!! Is ya'll sure ya'll ready for this shit? said Charlie with a serious look on his face. Pop's!! I been ready to step my game up!! said Freeze with money in his eye's. The first time I was kind of nervous to make that step!! but I'm ready now Pop's!! said Freeze ready to get money. But when we started telling people we had it!! They been calling none stop!! So what do we suppose to tell them now? Because I know when we start it's going to be booming watch!! said Freeze. Well all that sound good!! But it's a lot of shit going on in the game right now son!! said Charlie. What's going on Pop's!! We got a problem or something!! said Freeze with murder in his eye's. Son it's something we can't fix!! said Charlie with a sad look on his face. I went to my doctor yesterday and they found a bump on my lung's!! I suppose to still be there but I had to have this talk with you first!! I don't know how much more time I got to be here!! So I feel it's time for you and your right hand man to move up in the game!! Because it's nobody out here in the game that's on ya'll level!! said Charlie couching in a napkin. So I got some people I want ya'll to meet because when I die!! and ya'll haven't met them then your on your own!! said Charlie. Man you not about to die no time soon!! said Freeze trying to smile. See that's what's wrong with ya'll young nigga's today!! Ya'll scared of death!! See death can come when you least expect it!! So always be ready, So never be scared of something that's going to happen any ways!! said Charlie looking straight at Freeze. Pop's don't get me wrong!! I'm ready when it come, But a lot of mother fuckers coming with me!! That's on everything I love Pop's!! said Freeze. I understand everything you saying! But when that day come you have to leave your kid's or your family something!! said Charlie with a serious look in his eye's. And what I'm saying is don't live life bye the hour!! Now ya'll come on before it get to late!! As they rode Charlie was putting Freeze and Blaze on point on what was about to take place; when they pulled up on one of the biggest houses they have ever seen in there life. In the front yard was a pond that the driveway was wrapped around, with four dread headed nigga with A.K '47's and pit bull's on both sides of the front door. When Charlie stopped his car the front door opened to the house and one of the most ugliest nigga's Freeze ever seen in his life walked out with two of the most baddest bitches he had ever seen in Duval and walked up to Charlie with one of the biggest smiles he seen on a person gave him a hug and they started walking and talking. While Charlie and the dread was talking, Freeze and Blaze was in the back yard. When Freeze and Blaze stepped off the porch it felt like they stepped into a Safari. They seen deer's walking around drinking out the lake, while fishes was jumping around in the pond. Nigga this the type of shit I want out the game!! said Freeze with big shit working around in his head. Fuck all that petty shit these other nigga's on in the game!! I want this type of life style!! said Freeze. So when nigga's walk in they dam near fall out from all the fly shit you got!! said Blaze with greed in his eye's. Bruh on some G-Shit we about to have the game on lock!! I'm not bullshiting at all!! said Blaze. I feel ya bruh!! Every dollar I make going in the safe!! I'm not fucking off from this point on!! said Freeze while him and Blaze was looking at the ground's never hearing Dread walk up on them. I see ya'll like the house? said Dread making Freeze and Blaze look back and reach for there gun's but they forgot they had to leave them home. But the world isn't all about this!! It's about being real to what you believe in and loyal to who's loyal to you!! As long as ya'll keep them few rule's we'll never have any problem's!! But by any chance one of ya'll ever cross that line!! I'll cut your fucking throat!! said Dread looking straight at Blaze. Now on that note welcome to the family!! I look forward to making million's with ya'll!! O yeah!! One more thing! I don't deal with the law at all!! Kevin me and your old man been good friend's from over 30 years!! And I'm doing this on his face because I trust his word!! So just remember!! One thing and one thing only!! Your friend is your friend!! said Dread with murder in his eye's. Look sir!! With all do respect this is my brother!! And we have a bond that nobody can brake or mess up!! said Freeze. So if he can't come on this ride then I guess I have to miss this ride!! said Freeze dropping his head. See that's the loyalty I'm talking about there!! said Dread with a smile. Because no matter what the price was you wasn't going to let your right hand man die!! said Dread looking at Blaze. Whole up what you mean die? said Blaze not known what was about to happen to him. O! I'm sorry if you got me misunderstood in any type of way!! But if Kevin didn't step up for you!! You was going to die right here on my land and fed to the animals!! said Dread while turning around and walking off to go find Charlie. After Dread walked off Freeze and Blaze grabbed Charlie key's and left while Charlie stayed and talked with Dread. So what you think about Kevin little friend? said Charlie thinking he already knew the answer. Well I think he's a snake!! But I feel he won't hurt Kevin but he'll hurt the business side of the game I feel!! said Dread looking at Charlie. I feel you on that!! But he been ok so far! So we'll work with him for now but if he fuck up his ass is grass!! said Charlie. And we'll only give him what we think he can handle!! said Dread. But we only doing this until you get better right? Look bruh you must didn't understand what I told you!! The doctor told me I only have 6 month's too a year to live!! said Charlie looking Dread straight in his eye's. He said that the cancer had spread everywhere!! So I'm just going to ride it out until my number called!! said Charlie with a sad look on his face. It's sad to hear that my life long friend I never knew it was that serious, my prayers go up to Jah for you my friend!! just live your last days in peace and I'll handle the rest... On that note Charlie and Dread B.K.A Slikk parted ways and the game changed for Freeze and Blaze forever.

At the JSO station...... Everybody have a seat, the meeting will start any minute now. Everybody sit!!! I have no time for the lagging, we have dead bodies all over the city and the mayor on me so I'm in y'all ass!!! Now, I'm moving Detective Mack and Detective Mable off the coco street murders and putting Detective Willis and Detective Sappe on the case. We have a deadline to meet and I expect it to be in full order by that day. Now get on the streets and handle this murderer running loose"

On the outside of the law everything was moving like butter. When Freeze first package dropped, he got all the game he needed from rerockin to cooking. Freeze picked up on it so fast that Slikk doubled his package everytime. "Freeze" come check this shit out. This motherfucker look like glass! We going to make a killing selling point for point and scram for gram and I need all my cash" Bra, look calm down for a minute all the money aint good money!" I know bra I was just bullshitting with you" on some real nigga shit we have to give a little to gain a lot, so keep that in mind..." The whole time Freeze was talking he never seen the look in Blaze eyes". In the car Detective Willis and Sappe was going over their case. ""Sappe! I feel it's more to this case than what we looking at, Because it says no force entry and that's how our victims were killed. It shows me whoever did it must of knew our victims!" I feel the same way, but I read the reports and everybody they talked to said either our man is Freeze or Blaze. We have no solid lead on either of the suspects, so we'll keep our ears open to the streets and wait on our guys to slip when they do, we'll put the cuffs on them."

At the lake house Charlie was on his death bed. Everybody showed up to show their last respects to one of the realist O.G's they knew. Charlie laid in his bed and welcomed all his long time friends. But one of the guess stood out from the rest. And Charlie knew it was something bad for this guess to be here. So Charlie raised his hand for the guess to walk over and speck. Hello Mr. Charlie!! I know you don't need no bad news on your death bed!! But I feel you need to know this. And with a low voice Charlie motioned for the man to speak. Sir!! I have some very bad news to tell you on this day!! But your two boy's popped up on a murder case I'm working on!! said Detective Sappe looking at Charlie. What you mean a mur...der!! said Charlie couching up blood in a napkin. Well the Caption put me and my partner on it yesterday!! But the finger is pointing more towards your boy Blaze then Freeze!! But they can still bring up something on him!! said Sappe. But it's just finger pointing right now on his behalf!! Well thank you Detective!! That's all I needed to know!! said Charlie. I'll be seeing you on the other side of the fence. After all Charlie guess left the only people was there was his assassin and his nurse. Look!! I need something done real soon and fast!! said Charlie with murder in his eye's. What's up boss man? said suicide. Well I need Blaze took in care of asap!! I'm already on the job Sir!! said suicide getting ready to leave for the job. Every since Charlie was on his death bed Freeze put all his time in the game. Freeze bled the block all day and night when he wasn't bleeding the block he was cooking crack and cutting the coke for the trap house's; Things was looking good for Freeze he had half of the houses on the block. Which came up to 7 houses and a building with 4 apartments in it so Freeze had everything looking like the Carter with the family business. From the time Freeze and Blaze started Dread had move them up from 10 bricks to 30 bricks. So everything was good except the funny way's Blaze picked up over the last 8 month's after the sit down they had with Charlie and Slikk. So when Blaze walked in the trap house Freeze stopped what he was doing to rap with his long time friend. What's up bruh? said Freeze putting fire to his joint. I feel we need to have a real nigga talk!! said Freeze blown out smoke. Shit run your mouth!! said Blaze. Well bruh I been known you dam near my whole life and I feel we grown apart in this shit!! said Freeze looking at Blaze to see if he could see any type of flaw. So we need to talk about this before we move on with this job!! said Freeze still looking. Shit bruh on some real nigga shit!! I feel like you bird feeding me!! Shit I put in work like everybody else do!! But I get the short end of the deal and I'm getting fed up with that hoe shit G-Shit!! said Blaze getting mad just thinking about it. Nigga!! I don't see how in the fuck you can say some Hoe shit like that and still be looking me in my mother fucking eye's!! said Freeze thrown his joint on the ground!! You should be laying on your face with 4 in your ass right now as we speck!! said Freeze grabbing for his fire but he seen it on the table. But while Freeze was talking Blaze pulled out his 38... Bruh!! I didn't want this to come down to this!! And don't move!! It'll hurt me to flat line you!! I need everything you got!! said Blaze with his 38 pointed at Freeze face. Dam nigga I should've seen the pussy in you from the start!! said Freeze with murder in his eye's. Fuck nigga save that pussy shit!! What you want me to pull out my Voilin!! said Blaze hoping Freeze didn't make a move. Nigga I always kept it 4,000 with you!! But this is the way you repay me by spoon feeding me for all these year's!! said Blaze with hurt in his eye's. Fuck nigga you could've been hauled ass from the jump!! said a mad Freeze. But you in here doing the fuck nigga shit!!

But one thing I do know!! You is a dead man walking and don't even know it!! said Freeze trying to figure out a way to grab his gun. Nigga you really is crazy ass hell!! You the one that's going to be walking through that gate with that old man!! said Blaze backing up. Now I need the rest of that money and work you got in that trunk so let's go!! On the outside of the house in the back yard two sets of eye's was on the house and could see everything that was going on inside so when they seen Blaze moving they went into action. Boy this shit looking real creep!! That boy Blaze playing with his life!! But we need him outside under the porch light!! said suicide. Shit it look like they walking out now!! said the other voice. So come on let's move to the other side of the house so when he come out we can knock his block off!! said suicide. Ok come on before they walk out!! said the other voice. Fuck Nigga walk out the door!! said Blaze with his gun aimed at Freeze body. Nigga you walk. Before Freeze could get the word's out his mouth Blaze hit him across the face with his 38; And you better not say another word either!! said Blaze looking at Freeze holding his head walking towards the front door. As Blaze was talking he never seen the two people holding A.K 47's, But Freeze did; And rolled off the porch and watched the two Assassin's do there job. The first bullet hit Blaze in the hip making him spine into the wall catching 7 more bullet's to his torso.

Before Blaze body could hit the ground Freeze grabbed the bags Blaze had already packed and hit the highway. As Freeze drove, His brain keep going to Blaze and the two people he seen outside the house when the door came open, He couldn't figure out why they didn't kill him too. But then Freeze brain clicked back and thought; Shit!! Better him then me, thought Freeze as he smiled driving on 95. Everything was going good until Freeze seen something that he thought he would never see. Out the rearview mirror Freeze seen Red and Blue light's. Fuck!!! Fuck!! Fuck!! Dam I'm fucked up bad, thought Freeze thinking about all the money and work he had. A million thing's was running through Freeze mind, From running to shooting it out. But something just clicked in his mind and Freeze started to pull over. When Freeze pulled over he seen two body's getting out the unmarked car. But when he looked again he seen somebody he knew. "Suicide"!!! said Freeze as he got out his car. What you doing riding with the police!! Well this is Detective Sappe!! said Suicide. He's a real close friend to your father!! Get inside the car!! He have something to tell you about your boy Blaze!! said Suicide as they got inside the unmarked car. What's up wit ya!! said Freeze sitting down with the officer. Well like your Uncle said!! My name is Detective Sappe, And I work for your father!! Well your friend was working with us on a case!! said Detective Sappe looking straight at Freeze. We picked him up on the murder of Fresh and his baby momma Mocha!! And he put you on the scene!! said Detective Sappe. So we watched him for a couple of day's!! That's when we seen him about to take you out!! So that's what was going on with your boy!! said Detective Sappe. If your father wasn't on game you would've been a dead man!! In there face down!! said the Detective. You mean to tell me!! That nigga been a snake the whole time we been feeding him? said a mad Freeze. Look everything is all good!! said Suicide. We got all the lose end's out the way!! Now the only thing left is you have to turn yourself in!! said Suicide. We already got you a lawyer on the case!! So I'll holla at you in a couple of day's to let you know if you have to turn yourself in or not!! said Suicide looking at Freeze. So you saying I got to get locked up for a little while? said Freeze hoping that's not what he had to do. Well the lawyer say probably around 6 month's to a few year's!! But it won't be long at all nephew!! You can do it!! You a soulja!! said Suicide. And all the witnesses is dead!! So don't worry yourself about this shit!! Now go get you a room or something and keep your phone on!! said Suicide as Freeze got out the car and they pulled off while Freeze walked back to his car and pulled off headed to a room to get his mind right. As the night went on Freeze just sat thinking about what was going on around him. And to him everything was moving to dam fast down hill. He went from making calculated step's to being to predictable. And Freeze knew that was something he needed to change, Or he was going to be a victim in the street's to the next nigga with the same mind set he had...thought Freeze as he fell asleep. As Freeze slept his mind keep playing with him until he just forced his eye's open and made his feet hit the ground to start his day. Because he knew he had to dot all his I's and cross all his T's. So the first thing freeze did was make all his call's. And the first person he called was his old man. When Charlie answered the first thing Freeze heard was Charlie couching on the phone. When Charlie stopped couching Freeze started to talk. How you feeling this morning Pop's!! said Freeze smiling that he heard his father voice this morning. When Charlie heard Freeze voice his face lit up with joy. After Charlie couched four more times he went in his thought's and laced Freeze with the final step's to the game. I'm so happy that you called me my dear boy!! said Charlie still couching with a rag over his mouth. My time is coming to a end real soon!! I've showed you the game every since you was a youngster!! said Charlie couching more and spitting out blood into his rag. Now you've grown to be a very smart and wise young man!! What I'm about to say you really need to take this to the grave with you and always live bye it!! Hold up Pop's! Can I say something? Hell No!! I want you to shut up and focus on what I'm about to say!! said Charlie mad that Freeze would even try to stop his thought. Now you already know about your boy Blaze right? asked Charlie. Yes Sir!! said Freeze feeling bad. Good!! said Charlie. See that's the shit that get you killed!! Fucking around with inbreads!! They either get you locked up or dead!! Now in this thing you all call the game!! The only way you'll ever be on top of the game!! You have to be 6 or 8 moves ahead of the game and everybody!! said Charlie. And the reason

I said everybody, Is because you never know who with you or who's against you!! That's why it's very important for you not to ever fall victim to them nigga's never second guess yourself if your mind say kill!! Then you kill!! And don't let nobody tell you no different!! Because Blaze just showed you that snakes come all type of ways!! Now from what I hear you might have to do about 5 years or so!!! When Freeze heard that his face lost color but he kept it to his self and finished soaking up all the rest of game Charlie had in him. Now you have a option!! Either you go in there like a grown man and do your time and come home!!! Or you can go in there and act like a dam fool and throw everything away!! That's on you!! Now no matter what I say you still have the final call on your movements!! Now you got a lot on your plate to think about!! And I hope you use the smart side of your brain!! said Charlie known and believing in his only son. Your a very smart young man!! And if your as smart as I think you is! With the right team ya'll can take over the game one day!! Now get you some rest!! I love you my son!! said Charlie hanging up his phone to leave Freeze with his thought's. After Charlie talk with Freeze. Freeze couldn't do nothing but sit around thinking about everything Charlie just told him on the phone. And one of the only thing's kept running in his head was Charlie last words to him: Your smart and with the right team ya'll can take the game over! From that night on Freeze mind was like a chess game. And the only way a person can master the game; first you have to learn the game. The next morning Freeze got the phone call to turn his self in, so Freeze made all his last stop's to his close friend's Then he went and made his last stop to the Memorial Building in Downtown Jacksonville. When Freeze walked in and gave the clerk his name it seem like police officers was running from everywhere and the only words he heard was Freeze!! Freeze!! and not his name. Put your hands up now where I can see them!! said a officer with his gun out. Now you all can hold up!! My client haven't did nothing wrong!! He's innocent!! said Freeze lawyer. While Freeze lawyer was talking a tall white Detective walked up to Freeze. Look Sir!! said the Detective. I understand you have to play your part when you getting his and his father money!! Now you'll take him to my office!! After about three hours of sitting in the Detective office the same Detective walked in with a folder the size of the bible. Now Mr. Kevin or B.k.a Freeze!! Now what do you have to say about what the streets been saying about you and your friend Blaze!! Let me guess! You have nothing to say! Well your lawyer here!! So you'll feel free to say whatever's on you'll mind! said the Detective with a smile on his face. Man fuck you and that soft ass case you working on!! said a mad Freeze. So show me to my cell or let me go!! "O"!! I see we got a funny man!! said the Detective. But one thing we do know is your not going home no time soon!! said the Detective calling the transport officer to transport Freeze over to the county jail. After Freeze went through clothing change and I.d they sent him to the 6th floor; Now in the early 90's Duval county put all the knuckle heads from every side of town on the same floor so Freeze knew everybody on the 6th floor. For the first two days Freeze just walked around thinking how everything turned from sugar to shit... After the second night right before lock down came; Freeze was in his bed in his thoughts when he heard his name being called. The first thing crossed his mind was staying out of trouble. But survival was on his mind first and for most. But when Freeze looked around he seen a face he hadn't seen in year's since he was a jitt in (DDC). Dam Slim!! what it do my Nigga!! said a smiling Freeze. Dam bruh this is a fucked up place for us to run back into each other at!! said a smiling Slim walking up to Freeze to dap him up. What the play is bruh? said Freeze making small talk. Shit everything is good!! Just some pussy shit that's all!! said Slim. This shit is water under a bridge Bruh!! said Slim. But I've been hearing a lot of good things coming from your way!! You already know Bruh!! said Freeze. But when we touchdown we need to link up!! said Slim. We can do that! I got about 5 to do so get everything right for us bruh!! said Freeze still happy to see his partner. 10/4!! I got 18 months to do!! That's why they moving me because Lake Butler run on Tuesdays and Thursdays!! said Slim. That's what's up fam!! We don't need to pass numbers! Real Niggas always cross paths again!! said Freeze dapping up Slim while Slim grabbed his bags and walked out the sliding door. After Freeze and Slim crossed paths for the second time, Everyday felt longer and longer. Freeze lawyer kept coming with plea deals and offers. But Freeze took everyday slow until he got that right visit from his lawyer Hello Kevin!! said his lawyer passing him a bomb of weed and a lighter. Man!! Tell me something good DAM!! said a frustrated Freeze. Well they said the final offer is 4 and a half years with all the credit you've done in here!! said the lawyer known that was something Freeze didn't want to hear. Man what in the Fuck I'm paying you for!!! said a mad Freeze while he was standing up. I understand how you feel! But this is the best offer I can get for you!! said Freeze lawyer looking to the floor. Fuck that shit you talking!! I'll do 2 and a half!! said Freeze dead serious. Look Kevin!! They was trying to pin a murder on you and you talking about 2 and a half years!! Come on is you really serious Kevin? said Freeze lawyer lifting his head to face Freeze. You've already done 6 month's in here!! So you'll have to do 4 years!! And with the gain time you'll do 3 years and 8 months!! That will fly! It'll be over before you know it!! said Freeze lawyer. If you want to get this out the way I can have you in court tomorrow? said Freeze lawyer while he pulled out a blue form. After about 15 minutes of listening to his lawyer, Freeze came up with one of the most smarted things he ever came up with Man let me sign that bull shit form!!(Now a blue form in Duval is for a plea deal) Once Freeze signed the form and finished talking to his lawyer about the court date Freeze went back to his dorm and it was like a 1,000,000 pounds was lifted off his back. The next day came and everything went as planned but it seemed like after the court date time started moving extra fast for Freeze two weeks had passed and Freeze was on the bus going to Lake Butler, After the guard's searched Freeze and shaved his head bald they sent Freeze to the Wild Wild West!! The first thing the dorm officer made them do was drop there bags and stand at parade rest. After about 15 minutes of talking the guard gave everybody a orange hat. After three weeks of marching and doing push up Freeze was shipped off to Lake City CI. When Freeze got there they had him in orientation for about a month after that Freeze was moved to his dorm and he started his routine of pull ups, dips, and push ups. After the same routine for the first 2 months Freeze started walking around watching everybody movements and it was a young nigga that reminded him of his self, And the young nigga had the same routine everyday. And that was Played Chess. After

8 months all the holidays came around and people was getting care packets, So you knew what that meant... Robbery... That afternoon Freeze was in his dorm playing chess with a random person when Freeze seen somebody walking toward the table he was at; When the person walked up he knocked over the chess pieces. Look home team!! I just seen some nigga's brake in your locker!! When Freeze heard that the only thing that popped in his mind was murder!! Who was it bruh? said Freeze getting up out his chair. Them niggas in room 44!! When Freeze heard the number he went straight into beast mode. When Freeze walked in the room the niggas was still dividing Freeze shit when Freeze seen that he hit the first nigga. When the first nigga fell Freeze hit the second one with a two piece and was moving in for the kill that's when he seen the person that told him about these niggas hit the first nigga with a one hitter quitter. When Freeze seen the help he finished his job on the second person while his help finished the first person after what felt like a hour the guards came running in and Freeze and his help ran to there rooms and washed up. When the officers ran in they locked everybody down and went room to room checking everybody knuckles once they pulled out the beat up victims. After about 30 minutes Freeze seen them pull out the young nigga that pulled his coat on the niggas. Once they walked him out they walked to Freeze cell and rolled the door and seen the bloody t-shirt Freeze tried to flush down the toilet they grabbed him up and escorted him to confinement. After being in there for two weeks they gave Freeze and the Jitt 90 days in the box. The 90 days flew by and Freeze and the Jitt was back on the compound. It was rec time and Freeze was getting his shoes from under the bed when he seen a shadow standing over him right when Freeze was about to make his move he looked up. Boy!! said Freeze seeing a face he knew. Dam big bruh ease up!! said the Jitt. We already made our point in this bitch!! said the Jitt. That's what's up homey!! said Freeze dapping the Jitt up. And my name Freeze!! That's what's up!! And my name Bat man!! said the Jitt. That's what's up! But what made you help me with that little ordeal? said Freeze. Bruh I been peeping you out every since you first hit the rec yard working out then you started walking around watching everybody then you made it to the Chess field!! said Bat Man

telling Freeze everything he did since day one. And that's when you started watching me!! Shit bruh you crazy!! said Freeze known that Bat Man had just called him out. But I was peeping everybody out! And out of 1,500 people we the realist two niggas here!! said Freeze. Shit bruh at first it was just me at this bitch!! But birds of a feather flock together!! said Bat Man dapping Freeze up as they walked and talked, After that day Freeze and Bat Man was like Siamese Twins they played chess together, worked out together even gambled together until the day before Bat Man got out. Freeze and Bat Man was walking around the track. Dam bruh it's your time already!! said Freeze happy that his right hand was going home. Hell yeah!! But you only got 7 more months in this bitch!! said Bat Man trying to cheer Freeze up. Then you be back out there in that jungle they call Duval!! The next morning Freeze heard them call breakfast so him and Bat Man sat in the dorm talking until they called Bat Man when Bat man grabbed his stuff him and Freeze dapped up. We'll cross paths out there bruh!! said Freeze as Bat man walked towards the door. As Bat man was walking he turned around. Real Niggas always do!! said Bat man as he walked out the dorm! When Bat man left time seemed like it was going slow but it was Freeze mind going to fast until Freeze was laying in his rack thinking; About the first day he walked in this prison, Now he only had one more day off a 3 year 8 month and 23 day sentence. The next day finally came when Freeze feet hit the floor he walked to intake changed clothes. When Freeze stepped out he seen the prison car and that's when freedom hit Freeze. And from that point on Freeze mind was always 6 or 8 moves a head of the game.

It was a hot day in Duval County. When Freeze stepped off the bus his brain went straight into beast mode. So Freeze went to a pay phone to make his call but when he called the person didn't answer so Freeze walked to the front of the Bus Station and he seen a face he hadn't seen in years. When Suicide seen Freeze he knew that Freeze had spent his time wisely. His movement was different he even much had awareness. Then when Freeze shook Suicide hand Freeze had the grip of a man. So Suicide knew it was time for Freeze to be a leader, to take over and leave no prisoners. The whole ride Freeze was thinking about everything that he had came up with in prison but he knew he had to have some real street niggas with him, and he had to always be three places at one time. Suicide looked over and seen the look in Freeze face and knew what was on his mind Nephew!! said Suicide knocking Freeze out of his zone. What you did in there besides work out? After the slight smile Freeze gave Suicide he gave him the answer he was looking for. I played Chess!! said Freeze looking at Suicide. O ok!! So you think you ready to play me? said Suicide with a serious look in his face. And with a more serious look Freeze told Suicide: We'll see!! and went back to his thoughts until the driver pulled up to Suicide house and opened the door for them. As soon as Suicide door was opened him and Freeze was walking to the back yard and that's when Freeze seen a Chess board already set put. Now I'm about to see is you ready for the gift your father left you. When Suicide said that they was already at the chess board. Sit down nephew!! said Suicide looking Freeze straight in the eye's. This is going to show me how much you really want to get this money out here!! Duval could be yours!! If you pass this last test!! After about 30 minutes in the game. Suicide was up two pawns and a knight and was trying to put him in check. But Freeze knew that if he didn't kill Suicide soon, he was going to check mate him. That's when Freeze aimed both of his bishops at Suicide king. Then put his last knight to work. Freeze took piece after piece until the next thing Suicide heard was check mate. When Suicide looked up Freeze had a smurk on his face. So Suicide reached under the table and picked up a black bag and put it on the table. From what I see you spent your time very wisely!! Because most youngsters these days spend there time on some hot boy type shit!! said Suicide looking Freeze in the eye's. But from what you just showed me you've grown up mentally and a lot of people your age is either on that white girl or robbing old people walking out of stores type shit!! But I see from what you showed me that your ready for this challenge!! Now in this black bag is a number to a very good friend of my brother your father!! He's going to make sure you make it Freeze in Duval!! When Freeze opened the bag he seen some key's and a letter. When he picked it up he seen his name in Charlie hand writing when Freeze opened it the first thing he read was; Hello my Son... I'm sorry I left you when time was hard.

But I see you passed whatever test Suicide had for you if your reading this letter and this letter is for you my Son!! And the person who name is on the card his name is Brother Mark!! He's a good friend of mine, He's going to give you the key to the city! But you have to take the respect... Pop's. When Freeze finished he looked at Suicide with a tear rolling down his face and just walked to his room thinking about his father last words... The next morning Freeze hit the street's early he had already made the appointment with Brother Mark so he needed his right hand with him on this power move. So Freeze went to the place Bat man always talked about and the first place he went was The Plaza... When Freeze rode in he seen niggas walking around with A.K 47's, Crap games in the back of every other building. As Freeze rode through he seen Bat Man sitting at a table playing chess smoking a jay. So Freeze rode up. Nigga I caught you slipping!! said Freeze smiling. But when Freeze said that he had 5 guns aimed at his body. Bruh I'm never slipping!! said Bat Man getting up and dapping his right hand up and walked around the back of the building. So what bring you to my humble a bod? said Bat Man known it had to be some business on hand. Bruh when we was behind that fence you did some shit that most niggas wouldn't do and that showed me your loyalty!! So I'm here to show you my loyalty!! said Freeze looking at Bat Man. What that mean bruh!! What I did in the joint was from the heart!! Real Niggas Do Real Shit!! said Bat Man looking Freeze dead in the eye's. You don't owe me Shit!! Just keep it 4,000 with me at all cost!! said Bat Man dead serious. That's not a problem!! I got a meeting with my plug and I want you to be my right hand!! said Freeze looking Bat Man in his eye's giving him the run down. While Freeze was talking Bat Man just sat there listening until he stopped Freeze mid sentence. Bruh I'm with you all the way let's finish this in the car so we can ride!! said Bat Man ready to get money. The whole ride Freeze finished giving Bat Man the run down until they pulled into a church and walked into the basement and seen Brother Mark sitting at a clean polished table talking on the phone and motioned to tell Freeze it'll be a minute. After about 15 minutes of waiting Brother Mark greeted Freeze and Bat Man to the table once Freeze and Bat Man sat down Brother Mark picked up his cell phone made a quick call and

Freezing in Duval

sat the phone back down and looked at Freeze. Hello my god son!! I'm happy you made it home and did the right thing!! said Brother Mark looking at Freeze. So what's on your mind!! Well I'm happy to be out of that place! But my father gave me. Before Freeze could finish Brother Mark raised his arm. Hole that thought!! said Brother Mark as the basement door opened they could hear somebody walking in the room but when the person walked in he stood in the shadows. But when Freeze seen the face he almost jumped up but me wanted to see what part he play in this. Now we can start this meeting!! said Brother Mark. Now Freeze! This is my son Slim!! I've made him into one of the realist young niggas in Duval!! said Brother Mark. The only thing Freeze could do was stand up. Sir!! This is one of the realist niggas I know! His name Bat Man!! said Freeze while Bat Man stood up beside him and he finished talking. And the person you just introduced me to I been known him for years!! finished Freeze. That's a good thing there!! Because I need you all to take back over Duval for me!! said Brother Mark looking everybody in the eye's before he started back talking. All these random people keep popping up with my product! Taking my shit from my young niggas!! And I'm sick of all this bull that's been going on!! So I'm going to start ya'll off with 20 bricks of clean and from this day forward ya'll work for me!! Lets get money!! said Brother Mark as he got up and left the room. After Brother Mark gave Freeze, Slim and Bat Man the run down they walked outside towards Freeze Cadillac talking about all the future plans... Bruh this shit crazy as hell! The last time I seen you I was going to Butler!! said Slim smiling. So how you ran into my old man? said Slim. Now that's the crazy part about this shit!! My Pop's and your Pop's was close friends! So when I got out my uncle Suicide gave me the run down on what my Pop's wanted me to do!! So that landed me here talking to your old man!! said Freeze. Dam so your father was uncle Charlie! said Slim looking shocked. Hell yeah God Bless his soul!! said Freeze. Hell yeah R.I.P Unk!! said Slim drawing a cross over his chest. So what we going to do first? said Slim looking at Freeze. Well first we going to go to my spot and play chess and see who going to be the voice out there for us!! When Freeze said that Slim and Bat Man turned up. The first one to speak was Slim. Boy I'm about to beat ya'll ass!! said Slim laughing at what Freeze had said. On some real nigga shit! Both of ya'll niggas crazy as hell!! said Bat Man laughing walking to open the car door still talking. I'm a beast on that chess board! That's all I used to do when I was up that road!! said Bat Man closing the car door. Freeze just looked and got in the drivers seat while Slim got in the back and pulled off headed to the chess board. The whole time Freeze drove Slim and Bat Man was talking about there chess game and who was going to do this and that until Freeze pulled up in Suicide yard turned the car off got out and walked through the house and seen a glass chess board sitting in the guess room already set up to play. So Freeze pulled out a quarter and Slim called heads. But when Freeze flipped the quarter it landed on tails. Ok so now I'm about to see which one of ya'll going to play me first!! said Freeze. Bat Man which one you want? Shit I want heads too!! said Bat Man. When Freeze flipped the quarter it landed on tails again. So ya'll play each other and the winner out of ya'll play me!! said Freeze moving out the way so Bat Man and Slim could square off. When Bat Man sat at the table the game started. After about 45 minutes Freeze heard Slim saying check mate. Bruh this nigga was cheating! said Bat Man laughing getting up from the table. Nigga I told you that your game was trash!! said Freeze laughing at Bat Man still talking; So you are what you eat!! Nigga!! Fuck you I hope Slim beat the dog shit out of your ass!! said Bat Man. Freeze just stood there and looked at the chess board as he sat down. Freeze first move was his king side pawn; after about 44 moves Freeze was pushing his pawn for a queen. When Freeze got his queen Slim went for a stale mate but Freeze was on his game and just like that Freeze was saying check mate. Dam Bruh!! I haven't seen a game like that in a minute! said Slim. Shit I only play old people! said Freeze. So I know you sharp! said Slim. It's not that it's just I'm focused on this shit, And I got a point to make and it's not for No Bitch either!! It's to this soft ass game!! When Freeze started to talk Slim and Bat Man just sat at the table and listened to Freeze lace them with the track. Now this is how we going to do this!! As the street's going to know and the world! That we are one body mind and soul!! And we back in this bitch on that take over shit!! Now every one of us got our own way of handling shit!! So we going to go on every side of town! And we going to Divide and Conquer and that's going to be coming at these niggas all type of different ways!! We got to always think outside the box! And last but not least The early birds catch the worm!! Now that I got all that out the way! We got to put all three of our brains together and do this!! said Freeze. Because with our brain together we'll always be 18 steps a head of the game. After Freeze said that he walked over to the bar and fixed his self a water while Bat Man and Slim sat thinking until Freeze walked back towards them talking. So Slim!! What type of way you going to help with this movement? said Freeze drinking his bottled water! Shit I got some real niggas that's about this type of li!! I'll give them a call asap!! That's what's up make sure you get on that asap Bro!! said Freeze looking at Slim and turning around to face Bat Man. So what about you Bat Man? Shit my brother I'm happy you asked me that!! said Bat Man with a smile on his face. Nigga I got 12 of the most deadliest bitches in the state's! Freeze and Slim looked at each other because these was the same female's that had these niggas on there heals already. So when Freeze heard that he knew he had the head to the female's and he already knew they was 6 steps ahead of the game already. And they ready when I call!! said Bat Man still smiling. Freeze had a slight smile on his face. Now that's the shit I'm talking about there!! WE got this shit, now we got a week to put everything together and start making our moves! Now the first move is the Latin kings!! Now once we run them out the game! Everything else going to fall into place for us!! said Freeze. So now we got the plan now lets make it happen!! said Freeze as everybody got to work calling there trusted people for the take over. The next morning Bat man was on the block early. He had already made his calls to his lady's and told them to meet him at the apartment so when Bat Man walked in he seen all 12 of his lady's sitting waiting on him. The only thing Bat Man could do was sit on the sofa. I love ya'll lady's!! said Bat man. Ok I'm happy all ya'll made it here today!! We got some major shit going on in the street's! Me and two of my brothers on some take over type shit right!! And I'm taking all ya'll with me!! When Bat Man said that all the lady's face lit up with joy because all of them including Bat Man been waiting on there time to take over. So ya'll get up and get ya'll shit together while I make this phone call!! said Bat Man while his lady's was grabbing different guns and bags of bullets while Bat Man was on the phone with Freeze. When Freeze answered Bat Man gave him the run down. I got my girl's getting ready for the movement what's the play? said Bat Man. Now we got a meeting at my uncle house!! said Freeze. Ok I'll meet ya'll there!! said Bat Man walking out of the house telling the lady's to chill until he come back. The whole ride to Suicide house Freeze mind was on the take over and how everything was looking good on there behalf but Freeze knew that this was the right start to there movement. When Freeze pulled up he seen Slim and about 5 niggas in the front but Slim was talking to his uncle Suicide so Freeze got out the car and started to walk towards the back yard when he heard his uncle Suicide voice. Nephew!! When Freeze heard that he stopped in his tracks. I see what you got going on out here!! Just make sure you mow your grass to reveal all your snakes!! said Suicide turning around walking back inside the house. After about 30 minutes Bat Man pulled up without the lady's. But on he ride Bat Man had them drive a different car so 20 minutes after Bat Man pulled up the lady's pulled up then everybody sat down then the meeting started. Ok first we going to start with the lady's!! said Freeze looking at Bat Man. So when Freeze said that Bat Man stood up and got everything straight. Ok first these is Da Lady's not the lady's!! That's when Da Lady's stood up. Ok first we got Baby face!! Then we got Lil Bitt!! Then Slime, And Celle, Then there's Lola!! And Honey, And Mrs Butter, Gee, and Snow, And Tah, Then Yo'Yo and last but not least we got Katt!! And these is Da Lady's!! said Bat Man sitting down with Da Lady's. Now you Slim!! said Freeze looking at Slim. Ok bruh first we got my man Ice Cold! Then we got my nigga Big Jitt! Then Baldy! Then Rosco!! Then last but not least we got my man Greedy! Bka the can man. Ok now that the whole team have met! We can start our take over! The whole time Freeze was talking Baby face was imagining all the things she could and would do to him. Now the first move is on them fuck ass Latin kings!! They done came in with all the coke trying to take over Duval!! So from this point on we killing on sight!! We have a dead line to meet and we going to keep it!! Now everybody hit the streets and get to work!! We losing time sitting here talking so let's move!! said Freeze as everybody got up and made there move.

On the South side Miguel and Juan was sitting in their room going over their monthly inventory sheet when Juan stood up and walked over to the room window. Hey Juan what's up my brother? said miguel. But it shows here that last month we made close to 500,000!! Shit that sound good!! But I know it's way more money in Duval then that!! said Juan still talking, so we'll send our people out tomorrow looking! So get on that asap!! I will but have you heard about the murders that's been happening on this side of town? said Miguel. Yeah I meant to ask you about that!! said Juan. I have been hearing things but I haven't heard a name yet!! Do you think we have anything to worry about? said Miguel looking Juan in the eye's. I really don't know! Because we is making it hard for anybody to eat even our partners!! said Juan. So we need to keep our eye's open and our ears to the streets!! On Atlantic Boulevard Greedy was doing his ride through when he seen 4 king's bleeding the block. The first thing went through Greedy mind was how he was going to pull this off. All four of the kings was standing in front of a building across the street from a store; so after 5 minutes of thinking Greedy parked his car and popped his trunk. The first thing he grabbed was a old dickie outfit and threw it on with some old rags he threw around his neck then he walked over to a dumpster and grabbed some old wigs that was sticking out and a old dirty jacket and put everything on then walked and grabbed a old shopping cart checked his 2 snug nose 38's and went to work. On the block traffic was moving and the kings was moving with the traffic moving grams of soft and 50 slabs of crack so every stop was a nice pop. As the kings moved around traffic started to slow up so they walked back to there little stash spot to re up for the next rush that's when they noticed the can man coming their way. Didn't we tell that stank ass bum not to come back on this street!! said one of the kings getting the rest of the kings attention. Hell yeah!! Come on ya'll let's go teach this mother fucker bout being hard headed!! said the leader of the other 3. As the kings was walking towards Greedy they started picking up sticks and bottles talking shit about fucking him up. They never knew what they had coming to them until they was a few feet in front of Greedy. That's when he made his move. The first king got it the worst because he was lifting his arm to hit Greedy, But Greedy shot him two times up under the arm pit. The other three kings stopped and seen there brother falling from the gun shot. When they gained there focus they started reaching for there guns but Greedy was to fast for them. Greedy hit the second king in the neck and on the side of the head. Then Greedy just unloaded on the other two kings hitting one twice in the chest and shot the other in the back and seen him crawling on the ground. So Greedy reloaded his guns And shot the king two times in the back of the head. After Greedy made sure all 4 kings was dead he grabbed his shopping cart and walked back to his car like nothing happened. Crossing the bridge Greedy made the call to Slim to give him the update on what happened. On the first ring Slim answered. What's up bruh!! said Slim ready for the update. Yeah I caught 4 of them boy's slipping at the store!! said Greedy. That's what's up bruh!! Keep it moving bruh we got a lot more work to do! I'll holla at you later! said Slim hanging up his phone looking at Freeze. That was Greedy he said 4 down! That's what's up bruh!! said Freeze looking at Bat Man. It's show time!! said Freeze. That's what's up then Bat Man made his call to Da Lady's. On the first ring Baby Face answered. It's show time!! said Bat Man into the phone then hanging it up looking at Freeze. Everything a go bruh!! said Bat Man hitting his jay blown smoke out of his mouth. When Baby face hung up the phone she gave the orders. Ok ya'll that was Bat Man it's show time!! Me and lil Bitt going to the south side to handle that house we seen them kings chilling at!! said Baby face getting ready to go to work. And butter and snow going over there to Bert rd and handle them kings over there!! and the rest of ya'll get ready to move on call!! said Baby face getting ready to walk out the door with lil Bitt on her heals. On Fort Caroline road everything was slow but the traffic was still moving but the kings wasn't focused on the money they was focused on the two females that was walking down the street. When they seen the females stop walking and started talking to each other one of the kings walked up and started talking. Hello Lady's!! Do ya'll need help? Is ya'll lost? said the king looking at Baby face shape licking his lip's. When Baby Face heard that she turned

Freezing in Duval

around known her plan had worked. Hello handsome!! Our car broke down around the corner! And my phone don't have a signal! said Baby face in her most sexy voice she could come up with. But it worked because the king was all smiles. O I can help ya'll with that! Let's get out of this heat and go to the house!! said the king letting Baby Face and Lil Bitt walk in front of him so he could get a eye full. Once they made it in the yard the king was still talking trying to pull Baby face arm. Hold up little daddy!! said Baby face moving her arm from the king grip. I'm a Lady not a piece of meat!! said Baby face. We'll sit out here out here on the porch! And can my friend use one of ya'll phone! said Baby face. And with no problem one of the kings went to pull out his phone. Here she can use this phone!! said one of the kings looking at lil Bitt ass. And you can use the house to talk. As Lil Bitt was on the phone she walked around getting the full lay out of the house. Once she felt she had everything under rap's Lil Bitt walked back on the porch and gave Baby face the let's move eye. When Baby face seen the signal she went into motion. It's to hot out here let's go in the house!! said Baby face not giving the kings a chance to speak. But when the kings heard that there mind went straight to fucking something and they lost all focus on everything. Hell yeah we can go in the house!! said one of the kings holding his dick thinking he going to fuck. And we got a good ass A/C unit in there!! So as lil Bitt walked in she asked to use the restroom. I got to use your restroom and I hope ya'll got some toilet paper!! said lil Bitt walking to the restroom. Dam little momma! We not no nasty people in here! said the king laughing at what was said. It's down the hall way to the right!! Thank you Boo!! said Lil Bitt. As Lil Bitt walked down the hallway she seen all the room doors opened so see took a peep inside every room then she made her way back to the rest room. In the living room Baby face had all the kings attention dancing and bending over for them talking to them. So don't none of ya'll know how to fix a car? said Baby face still dancing for the kings. No!! But I got a old cat that fix my cars for me!! said one of the kings looking at Baby face work her hips. But he out of town! So why you said something about a mechanic then!! said Baby face looking at him with one of the most funniest faces she could come up with. While he was looking crazy the other kings was laughing until they seen Lil Bitt walking from around the corner holding two 40 cal's. When Lil Bitt first walked inside the restroom she looked around for anything that looked funny or out of place once she was done she pulled out her twin 40 cals and made her way back to the living room but when she looked around the corner one of the kings still had his hand under a pillow on his lap but all the attention was on Baby face and that's when everybody started laughing and Lil Bitt made her move. The first rounds of bullets hit every king that was on the sofa. But before Lil Bitt could kill the last king he jumped up and grabbed Baby face around the neck. Look Bitch I don't know what ya'll want but ya'll made the wrong mov. That was his last words because when he jumped up he never seen the ice pick in Baby face hand. So when the king grabbed her she just went with the flow until he made the wrong step or move. And that's when the king was backing up and almost fell down that's when Baby face went to work. When Baby face felt that she rolled out of his arms hitting him two times in the neck with the ice pick. Once the king grabbed his neck Baby face hit him 15 more times in his body before he had no more life in him. Once that was done Baby face and Lil Bitt grabbed their stuff and walked back to there car and pulled off. On Bert road Butter and Snow was on there job but there job was a lot harder because they had to run inside a apartment complex and knock off the kings that had a spot in the back. So as Butter and Snow walked around trying to figure out there next move they walked up on a whole in the back fence. When they seen that they posted up in the woods and watched the whole and all the traffic. But after 45 minutes of getting bit by mosquitoes they seen a Black Lincoln pull up and 5 Latin kings was walking towards it. But before they could make sure everything was good Butter ran out the cut with her two 9 mm shooting at the kings so when Snow seen that she had no choice but to make her move with her twin Uzi's. While Butter and Snow was killing the Latin kings the Black Lincoln pulled off. After Butter and Snow made sure that all the Latin kings was dead they ran back to there car and pulled off never noticing the same Black Lincoln following them. Dam bitch you could've got us killed with that hot girl shit!! said Snow looking at Butter with a nasty look. Girl fuck that shit you talking!! said Butter not paying attention to the rode. Them mother fucking mosquitoes was fucking me up I'm not paying you no attention so leave me alone please!! said Butter trying not to get mad. I was just saying!! said Snow rolling her eye's. As Da Lady's was driving the Black Lincoln was two cars behind them. The whole time the driver was following Da Lady's lil Hector was on the phone with Miguel. I'm telling you they just ran out of the cut and gunned them down in my face!! said Lil Hector smoking a Newport. So you saying you following them now? said Miguel. Yeah I'm waiting on that other car to pull up!! said Lil Hector with his eye's on the road but as him and Miguel talked on the phone Lil Hector seen a black on black mini van pull up on the car and the sliding side door opening up... As Butter was driving the hit keep replaying in her mind and she knew that Bat Man might kill her for fucking up the hit. But she knew she had to get her and Snow on the same page. Look Snow I'm sorry about that fuck shit I did at the hit!! said Butter cutting her eye at Snow. Bitch you can save all that friendly ass shit now I love my life!! You need to hurry up and cross that bridge because I'm going to beat your mother fucking ass!! said Snow ready for whatever. When Butter heard that she tried to put the pedal to the medal but she never seen the mini van pull up beside them with 5 Latin kings with Ak 47s until it was to late. The first bullet that hit the car went straight through Butter spine that had her paralyzed from the neck down. Bullet after bullet kept hitting the car Snow was running out of options. When she just grabbed the steering wheel so the car could go over the edge because Snow knew she had a better chance of swimming then shooting it out with the mini van. But before Snow could make the turn she needed a chopper bullet hit her in the back of the head... Miguel, Juan, Jose, Jesus, and Lil Hector was having a sit down while Lil Hector gave them the run down. Look like I was telling Miguel the other day! It's some new kat's that's named Freeze, Slim and Bat Man trying to take over our spots! said Lil Hector looking at the other 4 Kings. So why they trying to do that? said a confused Juan. So as Lil Hector was giving them the run down everybody was all ears but Juan couldn't keep his composer any longer!! Look since that's how they want to play trying to run us off by killing our people!!

said a mad Juan. Then we start knocking them off asap!! So Miguel and Lil Hector that's you all jog! Get all of our assassin's together and have them ready on call because when ya'll find out where they at I want them dead!! said Juan with murder in his eye's. Freeze Slim and Bat Man was sitting in the living room playing chess when Bat Man phone rung. On the first ring Bat Man picked up. Hello!! Yeah this face! I'm calling to let you know Butter and Snow went down last night! said Baby face. Dam!! How that happened? asked Bat Man. I haven't heard nothing yet but I did hear they got gunned down on the bridge!! said Baby face. So dam that was them on the bridge last night!! said Bat Man looking at Freeze and Slim. Hell yeah but that's all I was calling to tell you!! said Baby face. That's what's up sis!! But ya'll chill until I call with the next move!! said Bat Man hanging up his phone. Freeze and Slim was looking at Bat Man the whole time he was on the phone and couldn't wait to get the run down. Freeze was the first to ask. How everything looking bruh? Is everything alright!! Hell naw that was Baby face telling me that was Butter and Snow on the bridge last night that they pulled out of the St. John's river! said Bat Man. I wonder how in the hell that happened! They must have been bull shitting!! said Freeze standing up. So that let me know that the street's is talking. So it's our turn to make out move!! said Slim. And our presence felt, I know about a spot that the Kings use for a stash spot for there money! So we going to hit that house tonight!! said Slim while standing up passing the blunt while laying Freeze and Bat Man with the track. Look we going to burn that bitch down and whoever run out that bitch we kill on the spot!! Freeze eye's lit up like a tree on Christmas Eve. I like that and we need to bring out these big gun's because these King's using big shit on us!! said Freeze. But that was Bat Man specialty. Shit my little niggas hit a train a few months ago and got me about 20 AR 15's, 20 SKS's about 30 223's and a case of Mac 90's. So we good on the big shit!! said Bat Man making the call for the choppers to be ready on call. So since we got all angles covered let's make this move count. In Sin City Freeze Slim and Bat Man was posting up watching a two story house. Bat Man knew were a old house was that they can sit and watch the house where the Kings was at. Slim was splitting up the gas in two other containers.

While Freeze and Bat Man was standing by a window watching the house and all it's movements and talking. Nigga how you be known about all these crazy old creepy house's and Shit!! said Freeze laughing at Bat Man. See that's where people fuck up at when they be riding around chilling! See they ride looking at the house that look good!

See but I look at the old house because you never know when you'll have to use it!! said Bat Man. Nigga I'm not talking about all that!! I'm talking about this house!! said Freeze shacking his head. O!! When Slim told us about this house I sent Da Lady's to look for anything close like this that he can chill and watch this!! said Bat Man. That's what's up Bruh!! One thing I can say, You and Da Lady's be on point!! said Freeze still looking out the window. Shit we try!! As Freeze and Bat Man was talking traffic was moving in and out of the two story house. Inside the house Latin kings was walking around like factory workers. Some of the workers was answering the door while other kings was bringing in work, Up stairs kings was putting money in duffle bags. And bagging up new work getting it ready for the down stairs workers. This was going on for hours, But everybody had different shifts they had to work but nobody would leave the house. When it was time to switch they would have a different groups come in and take over. But it would always be 5 head Latin kings watching over everything and they was the only people aloud to leave. Because they moved money after every 50 thousand. And about 15 minutes later the bosses was getting the call that they had 50 thousand ready to be moved. But right after the call was made they heard screaming coming from down stairs. So all the kings from upstairs ran down stairs and seen fire everywhere.... After Slim finished filling all the containers he gave Freeze and Bat Man one and gave them the run down. Look we going to pour this shit from the back to the front and Bat Man stay back here and if anybody come out that back door murk them on sight!! said Slim looking at Bat Man. And Freeze you play one corner of the house and I'll play the other side!! said Slim walking towards the back door. Once Freeze, Slim and Bat Man walked in the back yard they could see the Latin kings two story house so once everything slowed up they made there move on the house. When they jumped the fence they poured the gas all around the house.

Once everybody was in there spot Freeze Slim and Bat Man lit there match and set there fire ring after about 2 minutes they heard people screaming. When people tried to run out the door Freeze and Slim was killing them on the spot, people was jumping from the second floor and first floor windows. But as soon as they hit the ground Freeze and Slim was killing them on the spot. Inside the head five Latin kings bosses was running for the back door but they only seen a flame but they keep on running. The first one to run through the flame Bat Man hit him with 4 bullets from his Mac 90 and unloaded the last 69 bullets from his drum in the door way... When the other four kings heard the gun shot's they tried to turn around but it was like as soon as they turned around bullet after bullet was hitting them until the last king that was standing stopped running and a bullet hit him in the middle of the forehead. When Bat Man walked in the front it was multiple body's everywhere. Dam ya'll boys wasn't bull shitting up here!! Come on let's go!! After the hit Slim went into beast mode, He put everybody to work And his first call was to his number 2 goon. On the first ring Slim heard the voice. Yeah Cold!! What's up big dog! said Ice Cold. It's your move! I need you to hit this trap on the west side! The kings use it as a stash house for there money so I need you to go over there and make it stop! said Slim into the phone hanging up after he heard Ice Cold say 10/4. After Slim hung up his phone the house phone rung. So Slim grabbed the phone and just listened to the voice on the end. I need ya'll to come pick this stuff up!! said Brother Mark. We thought he was going to leave it at the safe house? said Slim looking confused. He is but I want ya'll there to make sure everything is in place! So ya'll call me when ya'll get there!! said Brother Mark hanging his phone up in Slim face. Slim just shook his head and turned around to face Freeze and Bat Man. That was Brother Mark he need us at the safe house to do inventory! So come on! said Slim. And I got Ice Cold on that west side safe house hit!! And it's the safe house in Brunswick so come on! said Slim walking out the house with Freeze and Bat Man right behind him. Lil Hector was in his daily movements early the next morning picking up money from all the safe houses on the North and South Side. And his last pick up was in Lakawanna. When Lil Hector walked in he seen all his workers sitting on the sofa's smoking playing on there phone's with a bag on the table like nothing was going on. So ya'll just going to sit ya'll ass in here actting like it's nothing going on! Or ya'll don't got nothing else better to do with ya'll time!! said a mad Lil Hector. Once the workers got up and started moving everything they had just laying around up Lil Hector started walking around making sure everything was in place and in order. Once everything was to his liking Lil Hector called everybody to the front room. Once everybody was in the front Lil Hector didn't holed back. Look we have a real live problem on our hands! So from this day on we on high watch!! So that bull that I seen when I first walked in the house is a no go!! said Lil Hector grabbing the bag on the table and walking out and closing the door but he stop in his tracks. Ice Cold was in the back yard checking around when Lil Hector pulled up so Ice Cold waited until Lil Hector walked in to finish checking the window. After Ice Cold checked all the big windows he checked the bathroom window and it slide up so Ice cold jumped on the A/C motor box and looked inside the bathroom once he seen in was clear Ice Cold slide through. Once Ice Cold was inside he walked to the door and cracked it so he could here everything that was going on in the front room. When Ice Cold heard the door he made his move. When Lil Hector was walking out the house he seen a person running out the bathroom so he stopped to make sure he wasn't tripping but that's when he seen fire coming out a barrel but before Lil Hector could react he got hit 7 times in the body. The other kings was off guard when they seen Lil Hector fall and Ice Cold run from around the corner, They was still on the sofa when Ice Cold shot them with both of his 40 Cal's with the Extened clips. Then out the corner of his eye he seen a king in the kitchen reaching for something but Ice Cold was two steps ahead of the king and unloaded from both of his guns and ran out the back door. In Brunswick Slim, Freeze and Bat Man pulled into the farm house and seen a truck parked by the shed so Slim parked his car and they walked to the truck and seen it empty but the key's still in the ignition so freeze jumped in the drivers seat and back the truck in the garage. Once Freeze put the truck in park, slim broke the seal and lift the back as soon as slim opened the back door you could smell the purity coming off the bricks. Dam ya'll smell that said Slim moving his shirt wrapping it around his face so was Freeze and BAT Man then they started moving bricks. Half way through Slim walked to the truck and seen a note with all three of there names on it. So he opened it and read. And it said; I'm proud of you young men!! I see ya'll really is about ya'll business so I gave ya'll 100 bricks; and this farm house!! ya'll keep up the good work... signed B.M... After Slim read the letter he walked to the back to tell Freeze and Bat Man about the letter. Hey Brother Mark left us a letter telling us he left us 100 of them thang's!! Freeze and Bat Man couldn't hold back there joy. But Slim wasn't finish telling them the rest; And he gave us this farm house!! said Slim passing the letter to Freeze. That's what in the fuck I'm talking about!! Now we can make all the right moves in this shit!! said Freeze passing the letter to Bat Man still talking. So this is our foundation here so when we get back we start getting money and we start turning the pressure up 4 more level's we need everybody dead!! said Freeze looking at Slim and Bat Man and everybody had the same look on there face. Back in Duval Slim went straight to work making all his business calls then he started putting in hit's. And his next call was to Rosco and on the first ring he heard Rosco voice. What's up big homie!! I need you to hit this spot on the east side on Florida Ave! It's some kings running it I want you to make it stop!! said Slim hang up his phone. On Florida Ave. It was movement like always on the Ave money was coming from everywhere going to a yellow house with Latin kings sitting on the porch making the sales. Inside the house it was two kings sitting at the table bagging and cutting up slabs of hard while the other two sat at the other end bagging up grams of coke. Then it was two more kings walking around with choppers watching the two workers on the porch. Rosco rode pass and seen it was know way he was going to be able to do this hit without taking a bullet his self so Rosco drove off and parked on the back street and posted up in there neighbor back yard until night fall. Time moved slow but everything played in Rosco favor. Rosco seen one of the workers walk inside the house while the other one walked on the side of the house to pee. So when that worker finished and walked back on the porch Rosco ran up behind him and as he pushed him in the house he shot him twice in the back then Rosco shot the three Latin kings that he seen at the table then he shot the two he seen with the choppers; with the gun he was holding with his right hand then when Rosco was about to walk in the kitchen he seen a Latin king running from the the bathroom aiming a pistol. But Rosco shot him in the shoulder then two times in the chest. Then Rosco turned to check the kitchen and he seen the back door open. So Rosco checked to make sure there was no witnesses left then he ran out the back door to his car. In the parking lot of the Sun Set Inn Juan, Roc and Miguel was sitting in a Black Lincoln talking about all the hit's that's been going on around town. I don't give a fuck anymore!! It's war!!

They killing up all our people with these bitches!! said Juan with fire coming out of his mouth. Now Miguel you and Roc go out there in Sherwood and find out something on this Freeze and Slim shit!! Plus I got word that two of there bitches got a house on 6th and Perry on the east side!! So send Cisco and a worker over there and I want them to be tortured!! said Juan not thinking about what he was saying. But Roc was looking at Juan with straight disrespect in his eye's because Juan knew better then to send a worker on a job with blood. That was total disrespect to the family. Why is you looking at me like that my Brother!! said Juan just cooling off. You know why!! How you going to send a worker on a job with family!! You know that's disrespect!! said a mad Roc. I understand! And I'm sorry if I offended you or anybody else in the family!! But who else is going to handle this and do it right? And I can't do it because I got to make the money run now since Lil Hector dismiss!! said Juan waiting for a answer. Shit you act like I'm not on that type of time! said Roc getting mad at Juan. You already know what type of time I'm on!! Me and Cisco will handle that!! So don't worry about that!! said Roc getting out of Juan car. Freeze and Slim was playing chess when Freeze phone ringed. I wonder who this is! Then he looked and seen it was Bat Man. Talk to me bruh!! What the play is!! said Bat Man. Same old shit different toilet!! said Freeze laughing into the phone. But what's up tho!! Shit I'm about to slide through there these bitches getting on my last one bro!! said Bat Man That's what's up me and Slim just over here playing some chess that's all!! said Freeze. That's what's up!! I'm about to finish talking to there hard headed ass then I'm going to slide through there and beat ya'll ass on that chess board!! said Bat Man laughing hang the phone up. After Bat Man hung up his phone he could still hear Da Lady's talking shit about the new curfew. I done told all you mother fuckers ya'll need to be together in this house!! said Bat Man getting madder as he talked. Because this shit done turned up out here and this shit is for your own good not mine!! Everybody understood but Tah and Yo Yo they had to keep Bat Man going. Look bruh!! said Tah. We understand what you talking about!! But I got something to do tonight!! said Tah while Yo Yo Amen to everything Tah said. So we going to start our curfew tomorrow! Please and Thank you!! said Tah. Bat Man just stood there looking at her crazy until she finished talking. Bitch who in the fuck you talking to!! said Bat Man. Because I know dam well you ain't talking to me! You must be talking to yourself or that bitch standing beside you!! If ya'll bitches leave this house it's on ya'll not me! I'm not you bitches Probation officer don't get that shit twisted!! said Bat Man walking through the house making sure everybody heard what he had to say then he walked out the door Roc and Cisco was sitting in Cisco front yard going over there plan when a car pulled up. I wonder who in the fuck this is pulling up!! said Roc grabbing his fire. When Roc said that Cisco looked back and seen the car. O that's my partner come on. When the driver got out the car he walked straight to the trunk and grabbed two duffle bags and walked over to Roc and Cisco. What's Cisco!! Come on I got some Hi tech shit for you!! said the man following Cisco and Roc in the house when they walked in they seen guns everywhere Cisco walked over to the table and started counting money while his partner started pulling out devices from his bag. Roc was just standing there looking like a little kid in a candy store. What that is? said Roc. O!! That's something you can whole one of them hoe's pussies open and stick a water hose in it or something!! said Cisco partner. That's what' up!! So what that is? said Roc getting more into it. Look home boy I'm not about to sit here and explain everything that's on this table to you!! I'm going to leave a few of these toy's and I'm out of here!! said Cisco partner looking at Roc in a crazy way. Shit I'm going to be using them to so I need to know how to work these mother fuckers too!! said Roc feeling tried. Man ya'll chill!! Roc go in the kitchen so I can holla at bruh for a minute!! said Cisco known something was about to go down. After Roc looked at Cisco friend crazy he walked in the back so Cisco could finish his business. Ok bruh!! I know you about to look out for me but I need a few more items from you!! said Cisco looking his friend in the eye's. And it look like we beefing with a lot of bitches, So we need a lot of stuff to make them talk or something!! said Cisco. That's what's up bruh! I'll just leave a few more thing's for you!! But I know you asking for your people!! But you need to explain shit to him bruh I'm not one of these lames around here!! said Cisco partner. But it's not like that fam!! everything thing good it just a lot of stuff going on!! said Cisco dapping his partner up before he closed the door. While Cisco and his partner talked Roc was in the hallway listening, And as soon as Cisco closed the door Roc walked out the back. Dam cuz what's up with that fuck nigga? said Roc mad because he felt tried. Look cuz! Ain't everybody soft!! said Cisco looking at Roc with a serious look on his face. He's a cool ass cat he gave us all this shit here!! said Cisco pointing at the stuff. So come on lets go handle these bitches!! said Cisco grabbing some of the stuff off the table getting ready to walk out the house. On 6th and Perry Juan had two of his workers watching the house for any movement's or traffic... After Bat Man left the house Tah and Yo Yo packed a few bags and left the house for a couple day's because they felt they needed a brake. But the whole ride Baby face was calling Tah until she just turned her phone off and turned inside Popeye's chicken drive thru and ordered a family size box of chicken. After Tah and Yo Yo left Popeye's they rode to there house on 6th and Perry and pulled in and walked around the house to check for anything out of place then they walked in but they never noticed the eye's on them. When the workers seen Da Lady's walk in they made the call. On the first ring Roc answered. Hello!! Yeah! They just pulled up to the house a few minutes ago!! said the worker hoping this was his chance to shine. What do you need us to do? Good! Now ya'll just watch them until we get there!! said Roc hanging up the phone looking at Cisco. That was Heck! And he said they just pulled up so let's make that pit stop!! We only 15 minutes away!! said Roc as

Cisco mashed the gas headed to 6th and Perry… Inside the house Tah threw her key's down with something on his mind. And Yo Yo sat on the sofa and pulled out her nerve kit. And after about 2 minutes Tah could smell the sweet smell of the purple haze Yo Yo was smoking in the living room. After Yo Yo started to feel relaxed she walked towards Tah room but Tah was already coming down the hall. Dam that shit smell good let me hit that!! said Tah grabbing the Jay out of Yo Yo hand. Sis I'm sick of just sitting in a house looking at a bunch of female's! Now don't get me wrong! I love all Da Lady's! But I just needed a brake for a little while!! said Tah still smoking Yo Yo jay. You feel where I'm coming from! Yeah but pass my jay!! said Yo Yo reaching for her jay. You should have rolled you one! Girl fuck that! I just wanted to hit your jay but I'm about to go eat! said Tah walking toward the kitchen. Shit wait on me I'm about to put this jay out!! said Yo Yo walking down the hall.

Outside Roc and Cisco was checking windows but when they checked the front door it was unlocked. Hey cuz!! the door unlocked!! "Ok" let's wait until they go to sleep and make our move. Inside the house Tah and Yo-Yo was sitting on the sofa smoking when Yo-Yo phone ringed. "Hello" what's up bae? "Yeah" "ok" I'm home come on over!! Tah was looking at Yo-Yo the whole time she was until she got off the phone. "Bitch" who that was? "O" that was Tyrome!! Him and Punkin bout to come over here in a hour so get right!! "O shit" why Punkin coming? "Shit I don't know!! But you can ask him when he come!! The whole time they was talking, they never noticed the two sets of eyes on them. When the girls went in their rooms Roc and Cisco walked in the front door. Once they walked in they walked straight to the girls room… Both of da ladies had bathrooms in their room's, so both of them was in the shower. Roc went in Yo-Yo room and Cisco went inside Tah room.

Roc and Cisco already knew which one of the ladies they was going to torture, so Roc walked in the bathroom and pulled the shower curtain back. When Yo-Yo heard the bathroom door she thought it was Tah until the curtain flew open. When Yo-Yo seen Roc she went into action, but Roc was one step ahead of Yo-Yo and shot her 7 times in the body and walked out the bathroom. When Tah heard the gun shots she jumped out the shower and ran for her gun but when she opened the door Cisco hit her in the face and she hit the floor sleep. When Tah woke up she was still naked with a water hose coming out of her pussy and tape on her mouth and ears, once Cisco seen she woke up he turned the water on low and took the tape off of Tah mouth. Look first and last chance!! Who you work for? The only thing Tah could think about was what Batman was telling them, now she was paying the price for it. "Fuck you, kill me". "Ok" when Tah said that Cisco put the tape back over her mouth and turned the water on full blast, and watched the pressure from the water pop Tah eye balls out, then Cisco made sure she was dead by putting a bullet in her forehead and him and Roc turned the lights off and walked to their car and pulled off.

Freeze was checking all the spots when he stopped by Da Lady's house when he pulled up he seen Baby-Face outside crying on the phone, when she seen Freeze she dried her face and hung up her phone and walked to Freeze car. "What's up boo" said Baby-Face looking down and just started back crying. Get in ma let's ride! said Freeze. When Baby-Face got in, Freeze backed-up and pulled off. The whole ride Baby-Face just cried until Freeze touched her leg and made chills run down her body that made her look Freeze in his eyes. "Look" I got too much stuff going on in my life right now bae!! said Baby face. "What's up ma" talk to me! "Well" you already heard about Da Ladies!! "Yeah, I heard" answered Freeze. Then my father just died from cancer this morning!! said Baby face as tears just flowed down her face. Freeze didn't know what it was but he was feeling some type of way about Baby-Face, so he grabbed her head and kissed her ever so passionately on her lips. At first Baby-Face wanted to pull away but the feeling was so good that she went with it until they heard the people behind them honking their horn. When they realized they was in traffic Freeze pulled off the whole time thinking about that move he just made, it was a dangerous game but he was willing to play it at any cost Juan and Jose was at the Sunset Inn trying to come up with some better moves when the room phone went off. I wonder who this is calling this dam room phone!! Hello this better be the front desk!! No, this "Roc". I just tried to call your phone and it went to the voicemail!! "My bad" What's up? That job done we going in so call us if you need us.

After Juan hung-up he grabbed a Havana Cigar and pointed it at Jose. We making a move on them niggaz now we just have to find Freeze and that Slim cat, then we'll have the streets again!! said Juan happy from the news he just received from Roc. So that hit went well I see!! said Jose looking at Juan with a smile. Yeah that was Roc telling me everything was good so now we just need to move faster to make another move before they do!! said Juan getting nervous again because he knew things was about to turn up another level Freeze pulled up to the farm house with Baby-Face and Freeze knew this was another bad move but the way he was feeling he had to take that chance, so he walked Baby-Face in the master bedroom and showed her the bathroom while he fixed them a drink and rolled up a few jay's; when Freeze finished rolling the last jay he heard the bathroom door open so he turned around and thought he seen an angel walking towards him.

As Baby-Face walked, Freeze stood up and grabbed her and laid her on the bed. So many things was running through Freeze mind but his heart took over, he started kissing Baby-Face on her stomach then moved down her hair line until he started licking and sucking her cliques after giving Baby face multiple orgasms, Baby- Face crawled to Freeze paints and pulled out his manhood and looked at it then she started sucking and licking on his dick until he exploded in her mouth. After two hours of four play and fucking, Freeze slowed everything down and made love to Baby-Face for another hour. The whole time Freeze was making love to Baby-Face she was crying because nobody never made her feel like this. After making love Baby-Face went to sleep and Freeze stayed up looking at the window and he knew from that day on they was a couple.

The next morning Freeze woke up to the smell of pancakes, eggs and turkey bacon. Before he could get out the bed Baby-Face had his plate on the night stand and was bending over giving Freeze his good morning kiss. "Good morning daddy" "Good morning ma" What time is it? asked Freeze known it was to late in the morning to try and leave so he just went with the flow. It's 9:36 AM Daddy!! said Baby face happy to be waking up next to Freeze. That's what's up!! said Freeze walking to the bathroom to brush his teeth and wash his face. After Freeze ate;

him while Baby-Face took a shower then made love in the shower until they heard some movements coming from the bedroom, when freeze and Baby-Face heard that they went into action. Freeze had twin 40 cals on top of the dirty clothes hamper, down the hallway moving towards the corner of the hall, when they hit the corner they seen Slim and Bat man in the kitchen eating the rest of the food. When they seen Freeze and Baby-Face standing in the hallway naked with guns in both of there hands they could only laugh. But the first one to speak was Bat man. Nigga, I told you Slim! They was fucking didn't I!! said Bat Man still laughing "Hell yeah"!! said Slim crying laughing at the look on Freeze and Bat face face's. Nigga fuck ya'll!! Ya'll almost got killed with that tip toeing shit!! said Freeze still standing there naked. Nigga fuck that!! Ya'll need to put some clothes on!! said Bat Man turning his head. After Freeze and Baby-Face got dress they walked in the game room where Slim and Bat man was playing chess.

As soon as they walked in Bat man gave them the run down. Ok bruh we got some info on them kings!! A few of them be on the West side, So we need to make a move on them now!! said Bat Man looking at Freeze for the word. But before anybody could speak Baby-Face gave them her run down from her point. "I feel we need to hit that together bae" said Baby face looking at Freeze. So Slim and Bat man just looked at Freeze waiting on his answer but when he didn't say nothing they knew he was game. That's what's up bae we'll do that as soon as possible!! said Freeze looking at Baby face. But since you here and you never suppose to been here! You got to cook us dinner!! said Freeze slapping her on the behind. After everybody laughed Baby-Face kicked them out the kitchen and throw down a Sunday dinner. After Baby-Face finished cooking and everybody ate Freeze dropped her off, but before Baby-Face got out the car she gave Freeze a kiss and walked inside the house happy that she finally had a real nigga Brother Mark was getting all type of pressure from his plugs to the fact that he had to make a choice fast, but the whole night brother Mark walked around trying to make the right plan, but from every angle he came up short, so he sat in his chair and called Slim.

After the first ring brother Mark heard Slim voice. I see you stay on point my son!! The game love no one!! I see! But any ways!! I need to see you and Freeze one day this week!! "Ok" So what's up with Bat man? "O" Nothing I just want to chop it up with ya'll that's all!! "Ok" We'll link up around the middle of the week!! "Naw" it don't have to be so soon, make it toward the end!! "will do" After Slim hung up phone he had a funny feeling but he just brushed it off and finished playing chess with Freeze. When Brother Mark looked in his bathroom mirror he was sweating like he ran a race, he knew he probably just made one of his worst moves but his thoughts was short lived when he heard voices in the living room.

As Brother Mark walked around the corner he could see Juan and Miguel standing facing towards the hallway so he just played it off not known if they heard anything "So what bring ya'll threw here"? asked a nervous Brother Mark. Miguel sat down while Juan asked all the questions. "Have you heard about or of some people name! Slim, Freeze or Bat man?" When Brother Mark heard the names his face went pale, But neither Juan or Miguel noticed the look so Brother Mark played it off to the fullest!! I've heard the names! But never crossed paths with them! Why, what's the problem? said Brother Mark looking at Juan and Miguel. Well we been having problems with these bitches that call themselves Da Lady's!! They been killing all our workers and they killed Lil' Hector!! and I want them dead ASAP!! said a mad Juan. "How do you know it was them?" said Brother Mark. Because Roc and Cisco cleaned a few of them the other day and they had some of our clean on them, and I want to know how!! said Juan looking for answers. So what we saying is! We need your help on this!! said Juan looking at Brother Mark. It's going to be kind of hard for me to bleed the block like that Juan! said Brother Mark looking at Juan. The look Juan had on his face was the look of death!! You must of heard me wrong! I'm not asking you! I'm telling you!! Now I'm giving you two months to make this disappear or I'm going to make you disappear!!

Brother Mark just stood there in shock because he had to kill a son, because he knew Slim, Freeze or Bat man wasn't going to run, But he had one last plan, to try and talk Slim and Freeze out the game.

Because since Freeze came on board he flipped everything; Brother Mark wanted the money but he didn't mean it in this way because this was a whole different type of game; and he knew he could lose his life both ways. "Look" We'll see you in two months!! said Juan seeing Mark in a daze. Hello!! Hello!! After the second call Brother Mark snapped out his daze. What's up!! My bad I was just thinking about my next move, that's all!! said a nervous Brother Mark. That's good because we don't have time for games so you need to make a move as soon as possible. After Juan finished, Miguel stood up with a smile on his face as him and Juan walked out the house.

Inside the car Miguel couldn't wait to tell Juan the vibe he was getting from Mark. I didn't like the way he was looking when we was talking about Slim, Freeze and Bat man!! I noticed that too when I was saying certain things to him; said Juan; But we need to watch him more but we also need to find out something on this war because this shit looking real ugly for us.

The rest of the ride Juan and Miguel rode in silence thinking that if their thoughts was right it was a matter of time before their number was called....... Freeze pulled up to Da Lady's safe house and seen Baby-Face walk out the door like she was going on a date. The whole walk Freeze was just looking at her imagining different things when she opened the door and slid in the front seat. Why you looking like we going to a party or club or something!! said Freeze. Boi you crazy!! But the only way we can play this off! I have to go in the club and find him myself!! said Baby face looking at Freeze. So he just turned his head and drove off. Freeze was thinking the whole ride how they was going to play this, and that crossed his mind, but he didn't want to ask her, but since she insisted on doing the job he went with it. "That's a good way" but how you going to play that off known they know we using ya'll for the Hits? asked Freeze. "But they don't know who we is!!" said Babyface making a point. That's bout right "But I just want you to be careful in there bae!! that's all" said Freeze showing feelings for the first time in many years. Oooooo! That sound like love"! said Baby face smiling. Freeze just kept driving until they pulled across the street from the club "Ok" bae I'm bout to go in!! said Baby face. "Look" the whole objective is to get Jose outside the club so I can do my thing!! said Freeze looking to make sure he made his self clear. Ok bae!! "I love you" said Baby face getting out the car walking towards the VIP line and walked straight in.

Inside, people was wall to wall dancing and drinking. The VIP booth's was packed with Latin King's. You could smell the loud coming from behind the curtain. Jose was sitting behind a table with three phones doing his thing; until he seen one of his King's talking to a black woman on the outside of the VIP, and Jose knew that every female was suspect, so after he made his last call he made his way to the conversation. Good day beautiful lady!! How is everything tonight? said Jose looking her up and down. Baby-Face just looked at Jose because she couldn't believe how easy everything was turning out for her. Everything is good, thank you for asking!! said Baby face licking her lip's at Jose. So what are you drinking this evening madam!! said Jose. I'm not really a drinker! So what do you prefer madam? said Jose touching her arm. I just smoke weed! said Baby face. When she said that Jose put his finger to his chin in thought trying to figure out who had some weed that was in his circle. Then Jose came up with a quick plan to holed the lady off until he came up with some weed for her!! My lady!! Come in here and have a seat please until I get you the best weed in the south!! said Jose stepping to the side so she could walk in.

As Baby-Face walked Jose guided her to a table in the far corner of the VIP and pulled her chair out. After Baby-Face sat down, Jose fixed himself then took a seat next to the young lady. So Ms. Lady!! do you have a name? My name Jennifer!! but my friends call me "Jenn"!! "O" is that right!! So am I a friend Mrs. Jenn? Baby-Face just smiled and sipped her drink juice that Jose gave her then rubbed Jose on the hand, when Baby-Face rubbed Jose, his whole body felt a chill. "So" I take that as a "yes"! I don't want to answer so fast I need something to relax me!! Then Baby-Face took off her heels and rubbed her foot on Jose inner thigh. That made Jose stand up. "Ok" ok!! Jose picked up his phone and made a few phone calls. After the third phone call Jose had a smile across his face.

My beautiful Jennifer!!! I have found you the best loud in the south!! But we got to ride around the corner to get it!! I really don't ride with

Freezing in Duval

people I don't know so I'm taking this chance with you tonight!! said Baby face looking at Jose, "and sir"!! You never gave me your name! said Baby face. "O" I'm so sorry queen!! It's Jose!! The sound of his name made Baby-Face smile. That's a beautiful name you have there sir!! Thank you my flower!! Let's walk to my ride.

Outside Freeze was parked across the street from the club watching as Jose 745 was getting ready to pulled up in the front. When Freeze seen that he grabbed his 40 cal and crunk up his whip and watched Jose escort Baby-Face to the passenger side of his 745 then pulled off. Freeze pulled off behind Jose. Inside the car Jose was talking to Baby-Face about the grade of the weed she was about to get. This is some of the best grade of weed in Duval!! Do you have anything to smoke out of? asked Jose. "No"!! We need to stop by the store anyway!! because I need something to drink! said Baby face. Ok we can stop at this BP before we hit "10"! said Jose... As Jose pulled in front of the BP he never noticed the car following him because he was so focused on Baby face. Do you want me to get out for you? asked Jose. Naw! I got it I need to stretch my leg's any ways!! said Baby face getting out the car. Ok heres some cash for you my lady! said Jose. Baby face bent over and seen Jose pile off a hundred dollar bill. Here you go my lady! Help yourself! When Baby face stood back up she seen Freeze walking across the street towards the driver side window. When Baby face seen that she walked to the door with a extra twist in her step. That was the threw off to give Freeze that extra edge he needed. Freeze walked up to the driver side of Jose car and unloaded every bullet in Jose body, When Freeze finished he seen Baby face walking across the street headed towards the car so Freeze ran behind her while people was running to the Massacre in the parking lot. When Freeze caught up with Baby face she was in the drivers seat with the passenger door open for Freeze. When Freeze slid in the only thing he could do was shake his head at Baby face and the whole ride Freeze looked at her with a smile. The ride was a crazy one Baby face drove and Freeze rode in silence so Baby face felt she had to say something. What's on your mind bae!! said Baby face cutting her eye at Freeze. Freeze just looked at Baby face and smiled. Naw I'm just over here thinking; How you got that man to come out that club like that with no problem! said Freeze looking at Baby face smiling. You is a BAD BITCH!! said Freeze taking off his hat. Baby face was just laughing while Freeze was talking until he finished then she spoke. See bae that's one thing a woman got over a man! And that's a pussy and a phat ass! said Baby face. So what that mean! said Freeze moving in his seat to face her. What I said! Because most nigga's think with there dick not there brain's! said Baby face making Freeze relax in his seat with a lost look. For the rest of the ride Freeze just sat there and got some game from a female pro, But in every game something is subject to change. At the Sun Set Inn Juan was pacing the floor when he heard what happened to Jose the other night. Now he knew things was coming closer and closer to home. So me knew he had to move fast and make a move before Haviar showed his face. But the whole time Juan paced the floor Roc and Cisco just looked at him because they had some info on Da Lady's little hide out. After Juan sat down Roc gave him the run down on what was going on. Look bruh! One of Cisco people called him with the run down on them bitches!! said Roc looking at Juan smiling face, And we know where there hide out at; and we making a move tonight!! said Roc. That little info made Juan look at everything different. This war is getting to close to home we need to kill these bitches Asap!! said Juan with murder in his eye's. At the hide out. Everybody was out making moves except Gee and Katt they just laid around watching movies and smoking loud. When a commercial came on Gee got up and walked to the kitchen; After about 10 minutes Katt smelled some cookies being baked, So she followed hear nose in the kitchen. Girl I won't some of them they smell good ass fuck!! said Katt standing in the kitchen door way. I got you sis! Go make sure you paused the movie! said Gee as Katt walked back towards the room... Roc and Cisco was packing there torture bag Cisco grabbed a bag of wire and walked out the door with Roc on his heels. In the car Roc couldn't hole back what he had to say any longer. Cuz what we using the wire for? said Roc looking at Cisco. Because we going to make these bitches feel it tonight!! said Cisco with murder in his eye's. That's what's up! But how we going to work this? And what's in the bag? said Roc. Don't worry about it!! Just watch and see! said Cisco driving down every back rode. About 45 minutes later Cisco was pulling up on the street the hide out was on and pulled into a empty yard and jumped out walking towards the room window where the light was on at. But when Cisco walked up he seen the light from the camera and stopped Roc from walking. They got a camera on the side of the house! said Cisco pointing at the camera. So watch your step! Cisco opened his bag and pulled out some wire cutters. Then he walked on the blind side of the camera and cut the black wire that killed the view on that type of camera they had. After him and Roc walked around clipping the wire's on the cameras they posted up at the window and watched two female's eat cookie's and watch movie's Girl that movie was crazy as hell!! And I don't know what you put in them cookies but I'm hungry as fuck!! said Katt. I'm about to fry some chicken! You won't some? asked Katt. Hell yeah! This some good ass loud Bat Man got for us!! said Gee high ass fuck. I know right! And how many piece's you won't? I won't 4 of them little ass wing's you got in there!! said Gee laughing getting off the bed. Why you doing that I'm going to check my email! Katt walked in the kitchen while Gee walked in the camera room and seen all the cameras was down on both sides of the house. Hey Katt both of the cameras on the sides of the house is out! Come watch my back why I check this out real quick!! said Gee. Girl gone head out there ain't nothing about to happen to you out there!! said Katt laughing. Gee looked at her 40 cal on the night stand but left it there and walked to the back door and opened it Roc and Cisco was looking through the window watching all the movement in the house when they seen one of the females walking towards the back door. That's when they made there move towards the back door. When Gee opened the door Cisco grabbed her around her neck and pulled her out the door while Roc ran in the kitchen and hit Katt across the head and knocked her out and tied her up. While Cisco dragged Gee in the kitchen and tied her up next to her friend. Then him and Roc checked the house for anybody else then they walked back to the kitchen and Cisco pulled two cords out his bag and grabbed two pot's and filled them up with water and up both of Da Lady's feet in the pot's of water and plugged the cords up and electrocuted both of them to death. The smell made Roc run out the door, But Cisco stood there and made sure everything was good and before he left all the power on the block went out Freeze, Slim and Bat Man was sitting at the farm house talking about the hit at Da Lady's hide out. Bat Man was the first to talk. I don't care what neither one of ya'll say!! But I feel like somebody telling them about our houses!! said Bat Man taking a sip out his cup. Because nobody but family know about these houses they hitting! Freeze just walked to the window why Slim voiced his opinion. I feel ya bruh! But who do you think it is? said Slim looking at Bat Man. Because everybody that's with us is family we went through the struggle together!! said Slim. So it got to be somebody deep in the family that's doing this! That's just how I feel!! said Bat Man thinking hard because somebody was going to die about his Lady's. Freeze turned around with fire in his eye's. I don't know who playing these games but we need to get on our job before it hit us!! said Freeze. That's what I'm saying bruh we need to check everybody out from the top to the bottom!! said Bat Man standing up. And that's with Brother Mark but I doubt he'll play with us!! Shit I don't put shit pass nobody!! Me and Bat Man about to bleed the block and see what we come up with!! said Freeze dapping Slim up. And I'm going to holla at one of Rosco home boys that need a family! I'll keep ya'll posted on the play!! That's what's up just make sure everything is everything we got enough problems already bruh!! said Freeze while him and Bat Man walked out the door. The whole ride Slim was thinking about the hit and from how it looked to him all Da Lady's was suspect and he knew how Freeze felt about Baby face and if anything happened to her Jacksonville had hell to pay. As Slim drove he pulled in the Plaza apartments in the middle and seen Rosco talking to a young cat so Slim parked and walked up on Rosco they dapped up and Rosco led the way. Yo Slim this my nigga Trav! said Rosco watching Slim just look at him with a blank face. When Rosco finished Slim gave Trav the run down. Look I'm not about to sit and talk your head off!! If Rosco say you good then I'm going off his word! So if you flaw or any type of pussy shit coming from you then Rosco coming to see about you!! said Slim looking at Rosco and Trav; So I'm saying that's your problem! If he get out of pocket that's your job!! said Slim walking back to his car and pulling off... Thing's was

Freezing in Duval

looking ugly for both sides. Money was coming but the body count was uncountable; J.S.O turned up the heat but every side stayed solid to the code so the heat died down some. So a month later Brother Mark called a sit down with Freeze and Slim why they was at the farm house playing chess Slim got the call... Bruh this shit crazy ass fuck that was Brother Mark! He called a sit down with me and you what you think it's about? asked Slim looking at Freeze. Shit that's the fucked up part about it! I don't know what type of time that nigga is on but we'll find out!! said Freeze. And we need to move our people somewhere safe just in case he is flaw we'll be a extra step ahead of him! said Freeze known that his gut wasn't wrong. So we need to get on our job asap! I feel you bruh but who's to say he'll play the game like that? asked Slim. And he already know how we get down! His life on the line! said Slim looking at Freeze. You right bruh! You dead ass right! said Freeze. But we trying to stay 6 or 8 moves ahead of them! Because one thing I learned about this game was! You can't play every game the same!! said Freeze looking Slim in his eye's. Because in these streets everything good is subject to change; Because Greed is powerful and Karma is a Bitch!! said Freeze pulling the blunt. And the only thing Slim could do was think until he heard Freeze say something. So when is the sit down? asked Freeze. It's around 1:30 at his church!! said Slim. That's what's up! And Bat Man bleeding the block putting pressure on them Latin kings, So we should have something or somebody by the end of the week!! said Freeze standing up when he saw the time. So let's get ready to go see what we can see. Things was looking so bad for Brother Mark that everywhere he went he had a member from Da 4 King's and that was the point of the meeting with Freeze and Slim; Because Brother Mark knew he had to make a move and a fast one So Brother Mark passed up his seat without telling Slim and he knew it was a toss up, and he knew the game he was playing was sour. But Brother Mark had a good plan, a very good plan to make his 30 million dollar goal and run off to Brazil. Slim and Freeze broke Brother Mark thoughts when they walked in the door and sat in the two chair's that was placed in front of the lazy boy and looked at Brother Mark. Brother Mark just looked at Slim and Freeze and seen how they have transformed into a three headed beast with Bat Man and there moves was so swift to where he knew he had to play this right. I'm happy ya'll came on short noticed but I have a lot going on so I've moved off the seat!! said Mark. While Slim and Freeze was looking around noticing everything that was out of place but they just played it by ear. But the only thing Slim and Freeze could do was look because this was the sign they was looking for, So they just tried to get a little more out of him. So where you going? asked Slim. Well I haven't figured it out yet! It could be anywhere! said Brother Mark sweating from the question Slim asked him. But I'm not leaving now! Probably a few years from now but ya'll will be the first to know! said Brother Mark getting up walking out followed by his body guards. The whole ride from the church Slim and Freeze was in there thoughts because they knew if they didn't move fast they was dead. Time was moving fast for Bat Man dead line, Everyday Bat Man went into different neighborhood's trying to get some info but everybody he ran across didn't have anything for him. So he rode through the east side where he got the most info from so Bat Man started on Main st. Then looped around the corner to liberty st, once he seen everything was good he slide through Phoenix. When Bat Man hit Phoenix he seen movement and traffic going and coming to three different houses and everybody that was on post was Latin kings. So Bat Man creeped around the corner and parked in a yard that had a good view of all three of the houses and watched everybody movement's. The houses was well guarded every house had two Latin kings on the porch with choppers on the ground with towels over them. 2 and a half hours later Bat Man seen his opening when he seen one of the kings on the porch switched with another Latin king and jumped in a car and pulled off. So Bat Man waited until he passed him before he pulled out behind him. Bat Man followed him all the way until he pulled into a Krystal's drive thru. When Bat Man seen how long the line was he ran up on the passenger side and jumped in the seat with his gun out. Pull off fuck nigga!! Pull the fuck off!! Then Bat Man hit him in the head with the butt of his 40 cal. And that's what made the Latin king know he wasn't playing and he pulled off following the directions to the house in the muck where they torture people to make them talk.

As soon as they pulled in Bat Man went to work. The first thing Bat Man did was shoot him in both of his thigh's. The whole time the Latin king screamed Bat Man just looked at him until all the crying was gone then he moved closer to the Latin king. Look I'm not about to waste my time here with you! Who is your bosses working with? asked Bat Man listening to the Latin king cry for help. The whole time the Latin king cried he cried because he knew he was a dead man but he didn't like Brother Mark so he told Bat Man what he wanted to know. In a real low voice the Latin king said Brother Mark then started laughing. Bat Man eye's lit up when he heard that but he had to make sure. Holed the fuck up!! said Bat Man looking confused. What you just said!! You heard what I said mother fucker!! Brother Mark!! said the Latin King. When Bat Man heard that he shot the Latin king 6 times in the body and twice in the head. Then Bat Man jumped out the car after he gave it a good whip down then he called Freeze with the info... On the first ring Freeze answered and heard Bat Man talking to him. Bruh guess what I found out on my little through of the east side! But before Freeze could answer Bat Man was still talking. That nigga Brother Mark working with the Latin Kings!! said Bat Man brain on over drive. We already know! said Freeze. So we got to move fast if we want to stay alive! That's what's up come get me from the muck! And send somebody down to clean this mess!! sad Bat Man. That's what's up I'm on my way now Bruh!! said Freeze walking towards the front door. Haviar sat on the plane not believing what was going on in Duval he didn't know that his goal would be cut short by three young niggas, and the hurtful part that they was black. And he knew they was more dangerous because of there greed. So Haviar knew he had to move fast if he wanted to save his business. When the plane landed Haviar waited out front for his driver to pull up then 5 minutes later his driver pulled up and they drove to the Sun set Inn where he had everybody meeting him at. It only took the driver 25 minutes and he was opening the door for Haviar to walk inside the Sunset Inn. When Haviar walked in he seen everybody faces so he went straight to talking. Look!! I don't know what type of game ya'll think this is!! But I got pressure coming from the head bosses about this war!! And I don't understand why ya'll don't have this in order!! said Haviar looking at every face in there looking for a answer. And before everybody try and talk I only want to hear from one person and that's Juan!! said Haviar mad that he even had to leave his house for this bull. Juan whole face lit up because he knew everything was on him for now on and if this war get any worst his life was on the line. Juan was trying to talk but his mouth was so dry that he had to take a drink of water after he took his sip he started talking. Um!! We got some phone calls with some info!! said Juan looking at the table nervous. Look don't come at me with that little boy Shit!! I want names!! said Haviar feeling disrespected. Ok Ok Brother Mark called us with some information about 4 females they was using to knock off our people!! said Juan looking Haviar in the eye's. So you mean to tell me that they was using women to kill my men!! said Haviar sitting down can't believe what he just heard. When Haviar sat down every face in the room had shame on them. Look since they hitting all our work houses! Open up a couple more and see what happen!! said Haviar. And I want the Head of them Lady's and I want the head of who's over them! O ok!! We know his name! It's Bat Man! And we got some info on where they live!! said Juan hoping that would make Haviar happy, or at least smiled. That's good but whose to say he ain't playing both sides? said Haviar with a slight smile but still uncertain on what was going on. So what do you think? asked Juan now confused. It's not what I think! It's about how fast ya'll do this job! So I want Roc and Cisco to make this happen asap!! said Haviar standing up moving towards the bed. So ya'll need to make a move on that while I relax in my room. So I'll be hearing from ya'll soon! said Haviar as everybody started walking out the door After Slim and Freeze knew for sure that Brother Mark was a snake everybody started moving to fast until they lost sight of the real game; and that was survival. For a whole week different sides of town was getting hit to the point that people wouldn't come outside after dark so the police put a 9 o'clock curfew on the city and everybody that was outside was suspect, So Slim, Freeze and Bat Man knew they was moving to fast so they went to the farm house to go over there next moves. Ok we been the white for to long it's time for us to be the black and play the outside!! said Freeze looking at Slim and Bat Man.

So we can see what's really going on out there! Everybody people good so we will really see if Mark really that slimey to give them our family addresses!! And if he do that's when we make our move!! said Freeze looking at Bat Man and Slim the whole time he talked. That's what's up!! But how this looking; we better get ready!! said Slim looking at Bat Man then to Freeze. But Freeze didn't know his time was soon to come Thing's was looking so crazy that Bat Man had Da Lady's on high alert, He split the last 6 Lady's in three different houses so if the Latin king's did come it would be hard to track them down; but if you was a bad female walking or riding you was suspect to catch a bullet so every rule was being followed to the fullest So Honey and Celle was moving there stuff into there new place. When they was in the old house they didn't know they had so much stuff until they started moving, It took them 2 hours to get half way finished with there stuff. So Honey couldn't handle going without smoking so she grabbed her bag of goodies she got from the store and her bag of mango haze and grabbed two packs of white owls. After Honey rolled all 4 of the white owls up her and Celle went into another world.

Roc and Cisco had got the text with the new address so they sat and watched two of Da Lady's unpack a S U V for about 45 minutes then they went on the inside to unpack. So Roc grabbed his 40 cal and Cisco grabbed his colt 45 and they made there way towards the house. Cisco was the window watcher on hits and Roc knew he had a perverted eye for sexy women but he felt Cisco would play right and handle the business at hand since Juan life was on the line. But as soon as Cisco seen Honey in her boy shorts he caught a instant erection. And with that throw off Cisco never noticed Honey putting on her shorts grabbing her key's to leave After the third jay Da Lady's was higher than a pair of eagle so Honey got up and grabbed her key's and was about to walk out. But the whole time Celle was looking at her laughing because she knew Honey was about to walk out the door with nothing on. Girl you don't have on any cloths!! said Celle still laughing at Honey. When Honey looked down she couldn't do nothing but bust out laughing herself. Girl I'm so mother fucking high I can't even think straight!! said Honey. But I'm about to hit this Dunkin Donut! Do you won't anything while I'm out! said Honey grabbing some shorts to wear. Naw!! But we should go together! Remember what Bat Man said! It's hard for a bad bitch!! said Celle looking at Honey. I feel ya sis!! But I'm just going up the street!! said honey putting on her shorts walking toward the front door. So Celle finished unpacking while Honey walked out the front door Before Cisco could react Roc was already running behind Honey with his pocket knife out. Honey was so high that she didn't hear Roc until it was to late. Honey turned around to feel the cold steel of Roc blade. Cisco grabbed the key's ready to shoot anything out of place. Celle was unpacking when she heard something that sounded like Honey walking back in the house. Girl you just need to chill in the house and just cook you something to eat!! said Celle turning around to face who she thought was her friend. But when Celle turned around she couldn't do anything it was to late she was looking down the barrel of a colt 45. The first 3 bullets hit her in the arm's and one in the leg but two hit her in the head. Once Cisco finished shooting Roc ran pass him and went straight to there routine of looking around once they seen these was two members of Da Lady's they ran to there car and Roc called Haviar. On the first ring Roc heard Haviar breath on the phone so he started talking. Yeah I was calling to let you know that the info Brother Mark gave us was good!! said Roc hanging up the phone looking around while they drove away. When Haviar heard that he rolled out of his King size bed and walked over to the mini bar and fixed his self a strong drink happy because he knew as long as they had Brother Mark they would win the war and it would be over soon Bat Man got the news early the next morning so he called a meeting at the new spot and the only people was called was Freeze, Slim and Da Lady's. After Bat Man checked all the safe houses and put everybody else on game he rode to the spot and seen everybody that was called for the meeting and nobody knew what happened but his self so he played it off until everybody stopped moving around. Look ya'll this shit done got crazy for the home team! said Bat Man looking at everybody in the room. Honey and Celle got hit at the new hide out! So somebody telling somebody something! said Bat Man already known who it was so he put it out there. And I think it's Mark Bitch Ass!! Slim just looked because he knew it was true, But Mark didn't know about these new houses. Bruh I feel where you coming from! But Mark didn't know nothing about these new houses! said Slim looking at everybody that was there. I feel ya but who is it then! said Bat Man looking around the room. Freeze just couldn't stand to hear any more. Look man the way this shit looking we can't trust nobody out here in these street's! When Freeze said that everybody looked while he laid down the law. As of tonight we playing a whole different game! We on defense for now on! So we got to slow down and mow your grass to reveal all our snakes! And from this point on Da Lady's is on put up!! said Freeze looking at Da Lady's. But Baby face couldn't holed back any longer. Ok we understand what you saying and all but we feel like that's what's getting us knocked off being ducked off!! said Baby face. We feel like if we start rotating we would be about to see them before they see us!! said Baby face looking at Freeze. I understand fully wait you saying; but at the end of the day it's to hot out there for ya'll to be rotating around anywhere! said Freeze looking at all Da Lady's. So ya'll get back to the house and chill ya'll got everything ya'll need at the house so there's no excuse for anybody!! said Freeze looking straight at Baby face turning around to walk out the room Baby face heart just dropped to her heels as she watched Freeze walk away and sit at the chess board and moved his knight, But in Baby face mind she felt she had to show Freeze that she could make it with or without him After everybody left Freeze and Slim fixed there self a shot and sat in front of the chess board and played there game. Bruh I seen the way Baby face was looking at you when you was talking to them ya'll doing more than fucking!! said Slim looking for any sign's of feelings. What you mean bruh stop tripping! You know me you and Bat Man is like one soul! said Freeze looking Slim in the eye's. I feel ya on that bruh!! said Slim. But I am feeling that for real; but we from two different sides of the track's! said Freeze looking at his soul, She won't a family! And I'm not trying to be in the history books as another Boonie and Clyde!! said Freeze trying not to laugh. I feel ya on that bruh! But that's still your girl because you shouldn't have put your dick in her! said Slim looking at Freeze known he just hit a home run. When Slim said that the words hit home, So Freeze just sat there thinking while Slim picked up his phone and called in the hits. One the first ring Ice Cold answered; Hello!! Yeah this Slim! I need ya'll to close down them apartments on the south side called Caravan Trail asap!! said Slim hanging up his phone to see Freeze still in deep thought Ice Cold hung up his phone and looked at Trav. That was Slim you ready! said Ice Cold grabbing his Mac 90 with a hundred round drum. The only thing Trav did was grab his 40 cal and got up ready to go. Ice Cold looked at Trav gun and just laughed. You can't do nothing with that toy gun! Let me grab you something real! said Ice Cold walking in his back room and came back with a mini 16 with a seventy five round clip with two extra clips and all of them was full. And Ice Cold walked up to Trav and gave him his tool. Now you ready; now we need to make this move while everybody is moving around!! And one more thing! Everything must go! said Ice Cold as they walked out the door headed for the south side.

In Caravan Trail traffic was moving fast because everybody came to them apartments to get there pills and coke; people was walking around talking and hugging up on females while some people had grills out listening to music smoking and drinking not paying any attention to the car that pulled in and turned the lights off.

Crossing the bridge Ice-Cold laid Trav with the lick Look what we pull up follow my lead!!! said Ice Cold cutting his eye at Trav. "What you mean"? said Trav looking at Ice Cold like he was crazy. Nigga you heard what I said!! When I pull-up watch me After about 15 minutes Ice -Cold turned off the main rode and killed the lights. As soon as Ice-Cold pulled up he jumped out the car, the first 7 people Ice Cold hit fell with force. When Trav seen that he jumped out and followed suit. Trav ran up to a group of King's that was trying to get right and killed them all in on the spot. King's was running out of every apartment but as soon as they would run out they was falling. Every time Ice-Cold and Trav clip emptied they was reloading their guns. When they finished it was 27 Latin king's 10 niggas, 3 females, 5 dogs and a cat.

That move opened the eye's of everybody with rank in the city that made the four King's call Slim in for a meeting. When Slim got the directions he didn't know it was warehouses until he turned on the street. As he turned in front of warehouse "44" Slim seen cars parked but he only seen three so he parked and walked in and seen three of the kings seating at the table.(These wasn't the Latin King; These was the Four King's of Duval). Then there was one he knew from the East side; one of the heads of the CTC, So when he seen Slim he stood and greeted Slim... Hello my son!! Happy to finally see you all grown up!! said the King of the east side. We're happy that you made it here on short noticed! But we understand what's going on with you and your family! But ya'll can not kill Brother Mark until he cross the family line!! Everybody else is suspect, which is far game!! said the east side King looking at Slim with a straight face. Slim just looked at the three Kings, Until he snapped out of his daze, but this shit was getting to crazy in Slim eye's. So you telling me that the only way we can make a move is if he hit our family or one of us? said Slim with a confused look on his face. I didn't say all that!! I said family!! said the East Side King looking at Slim. Now ya'll just don't cross that line!! Once the East Side King said what he had to say all the bosses stood up and left. Slim knew that was the beginning of some shit. The whole week Haviar had all the Kings on pins and needles, trying to find out where the other Lady's safe houses was. So Haviar put the word out about the new spots he was opening on the South side.

Things wasn't looking the way Haviar wanted them to look so he opened up 6 more houses two on every side, and waited on Slim to make another move... Everybody in the streets was talking about the new trap houses the Kings was opening up, everybody was thinking disrespect, but Slim, Freeze and Bat man knew it was a set-up. So Bat man called a sit down with the last four Lady's. Everybody was sitting down but Baby-Face, she had her mind made up and all her moves, and the homework she been doing on this one house wasn't going to go to waste she had to show Freeze one way or the other. She listened to Bat man but in one ear and out the other tho. Look Lady's! This shit out here is looking real suspect!! We need all of ya'll to chill out here!! We'll handle the rest of this war!! said Bat Man looking at all Da Lady's. But Lil Bitt looked at Baby-Face and Baby-Face turned her head, so Lil Bit stood up and spoke her piece!! "Bruh" we really don't understand why we got to sit around and wait for somebody to come and kill us!!

said Lii Bitt looking at Bat Man with a serious look in her eye's. Look I didn't say all that!! said Bat Man about to laugh at the dumb shit he just heard. My words was ya'll need to chill I didn't say all that other shit or that's not what we trying to do!!! We trying to keep ya'll crazy ass females safe. So like I was saying! We going to handle this from here on out!! said Bat Man looking at Lil Bitt and the rest of Da Lady's. "But Bat man"! We feel like we can handle what come our way! said Lil Bitt looking at Bat Man in his eye's before she finished. Without ya'll help!!" "No disrespect,..." "Look"!! I'm going to say this one more time!! Ya'll bitches stay ya'll ass in this condo!!

When Da Lady's heard Bat man call them bitches they knew the conversation was over, So everybody went their own way. So Baby-Face walked in her room and pulled a box from under her bed and the first paper she pulled out was a pregnancy test that showed that Freeze had a seed on the way. The next thing she pulled out was a sonogram that showed Freeze was the father of twin little boy's. After Baby-Face wrote her not she waited until everybody was sleep and slide out the door going to make her name felt in Duval Co. After riding around for hours felt like all night, Baby-Face turned into the parking lot of a waffle-house, the first thing Baby-Face grabbed was her 40 cal but she looked around and didn't feel or see any danger so she put her 40 back and walked in.

After standing up for 10 minutes Baby-Face sat at a table and ordered her food, but she never seen the Latin King walk out of the restroom... When the King seen Baby-Face he made the call to Juan. Hello who's this it better be important? said Juan about to hang up his phone. This "Loco" I just stopped at this breakfast shop and seen one of them bitches!! "So what did you do"? said Juan on the edge of his sit. Nothing yet!! said Loco feeling dumb for calling. That's why I called to get the orders!! "Ok" How do you know it's one of them? said Juan getting out of the bed to walk around to get a clear head. Because it's the same one from the club with Jose!! said Loco. When Juan heard that the only thing crossed his mind was murder. "Kill her where she stands" said Juan making a cross over his chest and put his phone back on the charger and laid down known he was one step closer. When Loco heard that he walked to his low rider and grabbed his AK 47 from in the back seat with a towel over it, then he grabbed the hundred round drum and walked to the window close to Baby- Face... Baby-Face never knew that a baby could eat so much, so after her second waffle and an omelet, Baby-Face just sat there until she heard her phone ring. When she looked at her phone she seen Freeze face show, at first she didn't want to answer, but she knew if she didn't Freeze would turn Duval upside down so she mashed the answer button and put it on speaker!! "Hello, what's up bae?" said Baby face looking at the phone. "What's up"!! Don't what's up me! where in the fuck you at? said Freeze ready to ride. I stepped out to grab a bite to eat!! said Baby face. "And why"! Because we told your hard headed ass to stay in the fucking house!! said Freeze feeling his self getting mad by the second. You need to be on your way there because I was on my way over there that's why!! said Freeze. So take your ass home and pack some bag's!! You moving in with me!! said Freeze known that's was the only way she was going to listen to anybody. When Baby-Face heard that her eye's lit up. She never knew she would be hearing those words so soon so the only thing she could do was smile and jump up. Thank you baby!! That's all I... Baby-Face words was cut short when the first set of bullets turned her around.

When the bullets stopped Baby-Face was face down in a pool of blood and two blood clot's between her legs. Freeze heard the whole massacre on his phone and the only thing he could do was listen to the only woman he ever loved get killed and he couldn't do nothing about it but listen. When Freeze threw his phone he grabbed his twin 40's and ran out the door. When Freeze pulled in front of the Condo's he left his car and ran the steps to the 34th floor, when he opened the door everybody was sleep, so he ran in Baby-Face room and seen a shoe box with a note on it, and a paper that said give this to Freeze, when Freeze seen that cold chills ran down his body so he walked to the paper and read. Hello my King... if you reading this that mean something bad happened, I just wanted to tell you that I really did love you... and we would've been some real gangsta parents, with our two little Freeze's on the way. When Freeze seen that he screamed so loud that the other Lady's woke-up, but it was too late when Da Lady's ran in

Baby-Face room, Freeze pulled out both of his twin 40's and unloaded every bullet he had in the body's of "Lola" "Slime" and "Lil Bitt" when Freeze snapped back he seen the body's of Da Lady's. He tried to help them but it was too late. So Freeze stepped over their bodies and left out through the stairs.

News spread fast about what happened and Slim and Bat man was worried about the other people safety. They called everybody and everyplace looking for Freeze but nobody they called seen or heard from him, until they called Suicide then Suicide told them he was there but he wasn't talking much or eating. The only thing Freeze keep saying was he was going to make it "Freeze in Duval", So Slim asked Suicide would he talk with Freeze until they got there.

On the way to Suicide house, the car was quite until they pulled up on the gate. "Look Bruh" when we go in you do all the talking Bruh!! said Bat Man looking at Slim. Why you say that? "Because" them was my bitches and I know how Freeze feel about what happened to his girl!! said Bat Man turning his head to look out the window. And I'm going to ride with my nigga to the death!! said Bat Man still looking out the window until he turned around to face Slim. And we still need money so that's your field... said Bat Man looking at Slim and Slim just looked at Bat man and pulled onto the ramp and pulled around the driveway, then they seen Suicide standing at the front door.

When Slim and Bat man got out, Suicide lead the way. I don't know what happened I just know whatever it was fucked up my nephew bad. So look!! This is how everything going from now on!! "Slim" you is the voice of this!! Nothing happens until you say!! Freeze and Bat man handle all hits until his head get back on the right way!! said Suicide looking at Slim and Bat Man in there there eye's. Now ya'll take him with ya'll and finish this dam war ya'll got going on... when Slim and Bat Man got Freeze back to the spot he called everybody on their phones and let them know the whole set-up changed, And everybody had their self to keep safe and they had to make sure their neighborhood's was safe, everybody was accountable for their hood, And from that day fore; Everybody was their own killers. And move at there own risk.

From all the news Juan was hearing he had to tell Haviar the good news, and this was the time Juan felt it was time to move in.

When Juan pulled up he seen Haviar limousine, so he pulled into the open parking spot and headed for Haviar room.

Haviar was walking from the Jacuzzi when he heard movement in his bar area, and he knew from that sound it was only one person. I've told you numerous of times about just popping up, that's how people get killed!! said Haviar with his gun in his hand. "But" why shoot if you know who it is!! said Juan with a dumb look on his face. "See there Juan"!! You have a lot to learn!! You can never judge a person from the day before!! said Havair still drying off. What you mean by that? "Because"!! people feelings change!! "Or anything"!! said Havair not feeling like giving out no lesson. So sir what are you saying? said Juan really ready to know.

Haviar just looked at Juan and from the look. Juan gave Haviar the analysis. Well sir we have some very good news for you and the other bosses!! "Well" Da Lady's is over!! said Juan with a kool aid smile on his face. Haviar face lit up with joy from the sound of that. What do you mean it's over? said Havair mind still wondering if he heard right. "Well" from my inside sources, they tell me that they found 3 of Da Lady's dead in some condos downtown!! and one of our workers got that bitch who got Jose killed, at that waffle house!! said Juan smiling at Havair.

It's been over two weeks and we haven't heard nothing out of nobody so I feel it's time to move in and take what rightfully belong to us!! said Juan hoping Havair would let him work. The whole time Juan talked Haviar inside was doing flips to the point when he tried to talk he couldn't... but that gave Juan move confidence. So I'm saying!! We move in and kill whoever try to stand in our way or try and get in front of our money!! What you think? said Juan still looking at Haviar. Haviar was out his zone and the only thing he seen was dollar signs. "Ok" I want ya'll to chill right now! But next month we'll move in!! I just want to see what their next going to be... The whole night Freeze and Bat man rode to different spots killing and torturing workers, getting information!! But one of the workers gave them some good news,!! He gave them the info on who killed Baby-Face and his unborn twins... when they rode pass the house all the lights was off but you can see a small light or candle. So Freeze parked on the next block and watched all the traffic flow.

On the inside it was one candle and a flash light and Loco called all shots. And one of his rules was no lights, because he knew once your eyes adapt to the dark, you could see everything just using the moon light. He watched every movement everybody made in the house. After about 4 hours, one of the workers walked from the room and told Loco they was out of work, the only thing Loco could do was snap. "Got Dam" how many times I've said come tell me before ya'll run out so I can make the call to the safe house!! said Loco mad at he workers. Now ya'll mother fuckers just slow ass fuck!! Then Loco pulled out his phone and made the call.

Freeze was getting real restless waiting on something to happen, until Bat man seen a little jitt riding on a mountain bike towards the house. "Bruh" you see that? said Bat Man pointing at the jitt. What you talking about that jitt? said Freeze looking at Bat Man. "Yeah" I thing he going to that trap! And as soon as Bat man was talking the jitt rode in the yard and parked his bike and walked in the front door with his book-bag. "Ooh shit Bruh" Let's go!! said Freeze as his eyes lit up then he grabbed his Mac-90 and ran for the front door, when Bat man seen that he grabbed his SKS wit a hundred round drum and ran behind Freeze.

When Freeze ran to the house he ran to the front door and kicked it off the hinges. The first person he seen was the jitt, Freeze shot him 4 times in his chest, Then the next person he seen was Loco, he hit Loco with 9 bullets to his stomach, Then Bat man ran pass Freeze and cleaned everything that was moving in the house.

Slim just sat back and let everything play out, because he knew that Freeze and Bat man was going to make everybody pay who had something to do with Baby-Face and his unborn twin seeds getting killed and Slim knew they was smart enough to handle the mission, so he sat back and made sure everybody did their share in this war, and the first person Slim had in mind was Baldy.

Slim heard about some Kings that moved in "Pearl World" so he called Baldy with the update. On the first ring, Baldy answered with a low voice... "what's up Bruh"? "Shit chillin" said Slim still talking. I got something I need you to check out!! "what's up" It's some Latin Kings posting up in Pearl world!! I need you to go over there and make it rain!! said Slim into the phone. That's what's up! said Baldy. Slim hung up the phone and walked over to the bar and had a set at the bar and poured his self a shot of 1800 and took it to the head, after two more shots Slim walked to the picture window and looked out thinking more money-more problems.

Baldy threw this phone and hit the block, The first thing Baldy did was parked his car and walked for a bout 3 blocks until he seen two Latin Kings sitting in the front yard in lawn chairs, So Baldy cut through one of the neighbor's yard and jumped three fences before he was in the Latin King's back yard.

When Baldy looked around the corner he seen the two Kings chilling talking. "Bruh" this shit is too sweet!! These mother fuckers just let us come take their shit!! said one of the Kings. "Bruh we don't give a fuck bout nothing on some real G-Shit!! said the other one smiling. "Hell yeah" They can either get down or lay down!! said the Latin King giving each other high fives.

The whole time they was talking Baldy was sliding in behind them. Baldy had got so close that the first King he hit point blank range behind the back of the ear.

When the other King seen his home boi brains fly out he tried to run but Baldy hit him four times in the body then ran up on him and hit him two more times in the head.

As soon as Slim got the news about the two Kings in Pearl World he went to work trying to find out the last couple of pieces to his puzzle, he got a phone call.

The other day somebody was on the other end saying something about somebody baby momma doing charity work in "Ocean way" so Slim googled the address and it showed him where the center was. So Slim started his homework on the "Charity Center" for a whole week straight Slim was watching every woman and every car that drove in and out, then he'll go to the club and watch all the Bosses cars and it was a all black BMW that he noticed so he wrote down the license plate number and went home.

When Slim walked through the door he seen Monay laying on the sofa watching TV so he took his shoes off and walked to the poolroom and grabbed a pool stick and bust the balls. After 4 shots Monay walked in the room and sat down watching Slim play pool. The next morning Slim was up at the crack of dawn, the first thing Slim did when his feet touched the ground was thank God. Then he grabbed his 40 then walked to his twin sink's brushed his teeth and washed his face, when Slim finished he suited up and walked out the front door.

When Slim pulled into the spot the Charity Center was still closed... after about 45 minutes cars started to pull in. Slim waited until all the cars pulled in before he walked up to any of the all black BMW, the third BMW he checked matches the numbers he wrote down at the club. So he walked back to his car and waited until he seen people walking back out.

Once Slim seen the driver of the car he took pictures of her and pulled off... the whole ride Slim was thinking who would be the best person for the job. After about 5 minutes Slim called Greedy with the info... Greedy was up early the next morning. Greedy was used to wearing costumes to get close to his victims, but he liked to wear the can-man suit, so Greedy parked in a shopping plaza in the back and suited up then Greedy made his way around the corner to the Charity Center before any cars pulled up. When the first car pulled in the parking lot Greedy walked over to a dumpster and started pulling out cans and bags until he seen the lady on the picture. But when Greedy seen her she was out the car and in the building before he could make his move. So Greedy knew he had to switch to plan 'B'. So Greedy went back to his car and switched cloths and drove back and parked around the corner from the Charity Center then Greedy ran through the field that was behind the center and waited until he heard any movements from the front. Inside the women had a food drive for all the homeless people in the neighborhood. They would open up at 6:30 and close at noon. So Greedy knew he had 5 and a half hours for the lady's to lock the door from the people. Time flew by and it felt like 30 minutes but time was doing it's job; Greedy keep on hearing voice's coming from in the front but he didn't move until he heard older women voices laughing and saying there fair well's. That's when Greedy made his way to the corner and seen all the lady's walking, Then he seen his hit and made his move towards her. Greedy ran up behind her and unloaded all 6 of his 38 special bullets in her back then turned around while all the other lady's looked and cried but Greedy was running back across the field to his car and pulled off... When Juan got the news the only thing he could do was cry. The only woman he ever loved for 30 year have died from the hand's of a nigga. And was gunned down like a dog in the street's and this showed him that Freeze, Slim and Bat Man was playing or living by No rules; So Juan made all his phone calls to every Latin King with rank and turned the heat up full blast on every block and street. Juan gave them the names of different places he wanted hit and the name of block's he wanted hit and as soon as possible. After Juan finished all his calls he walked back in the family room where all the bosses was sitting and talking and Havair had the floor. But the whole time Havair talked Juan mind keep fading back to all the good and the bad days him and his wife had until Havair put him on blast. Excuse me Juan! We see you need a couple of months to deal with your family issue's!! said Havair looking at Juan whose mind wasn't all the way there. No no no!! I'm fine!! said Juan trying to plead his case. Please let me handle my own problem! Please I beg!! said Juan on both knee's. When Juan made that move all the other bosses looked at each other then they looked at Havair when Havair seen that he already knew what that mint. And Havair knew that Juan wanted to handle his own wife death but the other bosses felt it was time for Juan to take a little brake for a while. So Havair lowered his head and gave Juan the hurtful news. My brother!! We all feel like you need to take some time off with your family and let Miguel handle all the business and this war from here on out! So just take it easy everything will be fine!! said Havair now looking at Juan. The only thing Juan could do was drop his head in defeat because he knew when the bosses spoke it was the law. So Juan looked at all the bosses and bowed his head then walked off to his room to soak up in his defeat... Slim, Freeze and Bat Man sat in the living room playing chess when Slim got the text from Greedy about the hit. So Slim just looked at his phone made a little smile then made his move on the chess broad then looked at Freeze who was on the sideline and gave him the good news... Bruh that was Greedy who text me! I sent him on a little mission that I was working on; and I didn't know the bitch he killed was one of the bosses name Juan wife! said Slim looking at Freeze for any sign of joy or peace; but Freeze just looked back with the coolest eye's ever seen on a person and spoke; I'm not going to rest until every worker and every boss is dead!! said Freeze getting up and walking towards the patio and sat at the table rolling a blunt looking in the sky wondering what he would've did if nothing would've happened, Then another thought popped in Freeze head and told him that if he didn't get over the death of Baby face and there unborn twins soon, He would make the wrong move and that thought took Freeze mind where it needed to be.

When Miguel got the call that he was the boss he called everybody for a sit down, Because everybody had to know that what he said goes; so after 45 minutes different under bosses and top level pushers was at this sit down to see what Miguel had to say. After everybody arrived everybody took there sit and Miguel took the floor.

Slim just sat back and let everything play out, because he knew that Freeze and Bat man was going to make everybody pay who had something to do with Baby-Face and his unborn twin seeds getting killed and Slim knew they was smart enough to handle the mission, so he sat back and made sure everybody did their share in this war, and the first person Slim had in mind was Baldy.

Slim heard about some Kings that moved in "Pearl World" so he called Baldy with the update. On the first ring, Baldy answered with a low voice... "what's up Bruh"? "Shit chillin" said Slim still talking. I got something I need you to check out!! "what's up" It's some Latin Kings posting up in Pearl world!! I need you to go over there and make it rain!! said Slim into the phone. That's what's up! said Baldy. Slim hung up the phone and walked over to the bar and had a set at the bar and poured his self a shot of 1800 and took it to the head, after two more shots Slim walked to the picture window and looked out thinking more money-more problems.

Baldy threw this phone and hit the block, The first thing Baldy did was parked his car and walked for a bout 3 blocks until he seen two Latin Kings sitting in the front yard in lawn chairs, So Baldy cut through one of the neighbor's yard and jumped three fences before he was in the Latin King's back yard.

When Baldy looked around the corner he seen the two Kings chilling talking. "Bruh" this shit is too sweet!! These mother fuckers just let us come take their shit!! said one of the Kings. "Bruh we don't give a fuck bout nothing on some real G-Shit!! said the other one smiling. "Hell yeah" They can either get down or lay down!! said the Latin King giving each other high fives.

The whole time they was talking Baldy was sliding in behind them. Baldy had got so close that the first King he hit point blank range behind the back of the ear.

When the other King seen his home boi brains fly out he tried to run but Baldy hit him four times in the body then ran up on him and hit him two more times in the head.

As soon as Slim got the news about the two Kings in Pearl World he went to work trying to find out the last couple of pieces to his puzzle, he got a phone call.

The other day somebody was on the other end saying something about somebody baby momma doing charity work in "Ocean way" so Slim googled the address and it showed him where the center was. So Slim started his homework on the "Charity Center" for a whole week straight Slim was watching every woman and every car that drove in and out, then he'll go to the club and watch all the Bosses cars and it was a all black BMW that he noticed so he wrote down the license plate number and went home.

When Slim walked through the door he seen Monay laying on the sofa watching TV so he took his shoes off and walked to the poolroom and grabbed a pool stick and bust the balls. After 4 shots Monay walked in the room and sat down watching Slim play pool. The next morning Slim was up at the crack of dawn, the first thing Slim did when his feet touched the ground was thank God. Then he grabbed his 40 then walked to his twin sink's brushed his teeth and washed his face, when Slim finished he suited up and walked out the front door.

When Slim pulled into the spot the Charity Center was still closed... after about 45 minutes cars started to pull in. Slim waited until all the cars pulled in before he walked up to any of the all black BMW, the third BMW he checked matches the numbers he wrote down at the club. So he walked back to his car and waited until he seen people walking back out.

Once Slim seen the driver of the car he took pictures of her and pulled off... the whole ride Slim was thinking who would be the best person for the job. After about 5 minutes Slim called Greedy with the info... Greedy was up early the next morning. Greedy was used to wearing costumes to get close to his victims, but he liked to wear the can-man suit, so Greedy parked in a shopping plaza in the back and suited up then Greedy made his way around the corner to the Charity Center before any cars pulled up. When the first car pulled in the parking lot Greedy walked over to a dumpster and started pulling out cans and bags until he seen the lady on the picture. But when Greedy seen her she was out the car and in the building before he could make his move. So Greedy knew he had to switch to plan 'B'. So Greedy went back to his car and switched cloths and drove back and parked around the corner from the Charity Center then Greedy ran through the field that was behind the center and waited until he heard any movements from the front. Inside the women had a food drive for all the homeless people in the neighborhood. They would open up at 6:30 and close at noon. So Greedy knew he had 5 and a half hours for the lady's to lock the door from the people. Time flew by and it felt like 30 minutes but time was doing it's job; Greedy keep on hearing voice's coming from in the front but he didn't move until he heard older women voices laughing and saying there fair well's. That's when Greedy made his way to the corner and seen all the lady's walking, Then he seen his hit and made his move towards her. Greedy ran up behind her and unloaded all 6 of his 38 special bullets in her back then turned around while all the other lady's looked and cried and shot their way then ran back across the field to his car and pulled off.

When Juan got the news the only thing he could do was cry. The only woman he ever loved for 30 year have died from the hand's of a nigga. And was gunned down like a dog in the street's and this showed him that Freeze, Slim and Bat Man was playing or living by No rules; So Juan made all his phone calls to every Latin King with rank and turned the heat up full blast on every block and street. Juan gave them the names of different places he wanted hit and the name of block's he wanted hit and as soon as possible. After Juan finished all his calls he walked back in the family room where all the bosses was sitting and talking and Havair had the floor. But the whole time Havair talked Juan mind keep fading back to all the good and the bad days him and his wife had until Havair put him on blast. Excuse me Juan! We see you need a couple of months to deal with your family issue's!! said Havair looking at Juan whose mind wasn't all the way there. No no no!! I'm fine!! said Juan trying to plead his case. Please let me handle my own problem! Please I beg!! said Juan on both knee's. When Juan made that move all the other bosses looked at each other then they looked at Havair when Havair seen that he already knew what that mint. And Havair knew that Juan wanted to handle his own wife death but the other bosses felt it was time for Juan to take a little brake for a while. So Havair lowered his head and gave Juan the hurtful news. My brother!! We all feel like you need to take some time off with your family and let Miguel handle all the business and this war from here on out! So just take it easy everything will be fine!! said Havair now looking at Juan. The only thing Juan could do was drop his head in defeat because he knew when the bosses spoke it was the law. So Juan looked at all the bosses and bowed his head then walked off to his room to soak up in his defeat... Slim, Freeze and Bat Man sat in the living room playing chess when Slim got the text from Greedy about the hit. So Slim just looked at his phone made a little smile then made his move on the chess broad then looked at Freeze who was on the sideline and gave him the good news... Bruh that was Greedy who text me! I sent him on a little mission that I was working on; and I didn't know the bitch he killed was one of the bosses name Juan wife! said Slim looking at Freeze for any sign of joy or peace; but Freeze just looked back with the coolest eye's ever seen on a person and spoke; I'm not going to rest until every worker and every boss is dead!! said Freeze getting up and walking towards the patio and sat at the table rolling a blunt looking in the sky wondering what he would've did if nothing would've happened, Then another thought popped in Freeze head and told him that if he didn't get over the death of Baby face and there unborn twins soon, He would make the wrong move and that thought took Freeze mind where it needed to be.

When Miguel got the call that he was the boss he called everybody for a sit down, Because everybody had to know that what he said goes; so after 45 minutes different under bosses and top level pushers was at this sit down to see what Miguel had to say. After everybody arrived everybody took there sit and Miguel took the floor.

Now everybody settle down!! said Miguel looking around the room at every face. I'm going to make this short and sweet! I got the call from Havair this morning and I'm running the show from here on out! said Miguel looking around the room to make sure everybody was on the same page or close to it. So with that being said, I got some issue's in Washington Height's it need dealt wit asap!! said Miguel talking like he was the king and everybody else was his servant's. Roc and Cisco just looked at each other wit there mouth's open until Roc just stood up and addressed Miguel. Look! I understand how you feel with your new found power and all!! But that was my sister-n-law that Freeze, Slim and that mother fucking Bat Man gunned down! So fuck that shit you talking about! said Roc looking Miguel in his eye's. And we had already got the phone call before he was striped of his duties! So we going to handle everything he asked of us! Then we'll do what ever that is you was talking about! Look I don't give a fuck what ya'll doing or what ya'll talking about! But my word is the Law! said Miguel getting mad as he talked. Now I'm going to text every one of ya'll the information in two day's and I don't want No Bull Shit!! As Miguel walked to his back room everybody had a sour look on there face because they knew everything was going to go down hill that Miguel was in the seat In Washington Height's things was slow but traffic was still coming so money was being made; so Ice Cold and his savages was walking to different apartment's checking on work and money until Ice Cold ran into a female he used to fuck back in the day's so he stopped and chopped it up with her; while his savages played the field Roc woke up to the sound of his children running around the house playing while his baby momma cooked breakfast and screamed at the kid's every 5 minutes to sit down but the children was just happy to see there father so they keep jumping on the bed until Roc grabbed his youngest little girl and rolled around the bed with her while the other to jumped around laughing and playing that went on until Roc rolled out of the bed and ran to the bathroom and locked the door. After Roc brushed his teeth and washed his face he walked to the kitchen and sat at the table and watched his baby momma finish cooking breakfast. The whole time Roc was at the table the mother of his children was thinking about her children father and that she was happy that he was safe, because her and there children had to cherish every second minute and hour they have with him; because he think she don't know that's it's him and the rest of his friend's that's getting everybody killed in there circle so it was time for herself to turn up, After she fed Roc and the girls. She got the girls ready for school she cleaned the kitchen and walked towards there bedroom getting undressed as she walked. When she turned the corner for the room she seen Roc standing there in his thought's. Baby I know you just not about to leave us! said his baby momma with one leg on a chair that was by the door playing with herself looking at Roc turn around. When Roc seen that his jaw's dropped. That was the response she was looking for, she walked over and unzipped Roc pants and went to work the feeling was so good that Roc lift her and bent her over and worked her from the back for about 45 minutes before he nutted inside of her and laid on the bed but his baby momma seen he was still hard so she crawled where Roc was laying and licked on his stick until he came in her mouth and went to sleep; when she seen he was sleep she just smiled known that she had him for a few more hours. After about 2 and a half hour's of much needed rest Roc woke up to the smell of taco's and his baby momma walking a plate of food on a tray wit a flower in a small vase in the room and putting it on his lap. Once Roc started eating she let her feelings flow. Baby I understand that you have a job to do! But wouldn't you think that the girls would be happy to see mommy and daddy here when they come home from school? said Roc baby momma looking wit her fingers crossed. Roc just looked at his baby momma and thought how Miguel was talking to him and his crew; and just to show Miguel who was boss Roc mind was made. Roc moved the tray off his lap and grabbed his baby momma and kissed her on her lips. Baby I changed my mind! I'm going to stay home for the rest of this week and chill with you and the babies! Now let me make all my phone calls! said Roc grabbing his phone getting out the bed walking in the back room talking on the phone and the only thing she heard was Roc telling some workers to ride through Washington Height's and make it rain then the door closed.

After Ice Cold finished doing his walk through he called every worker and chopper thrower to be on point because things was looking crazy around town plus Ice Cold felt his team was starting to relax. So Ice Cold had 4 of his chopper throwers stand in the front cut 4 in the middle and 4 posted up in the back so if anybody rode through on some fuck shit they wouldn't make it out.

After Roc made the calls to the workers they suited up and headed for Washington Height's. Around mid night Ice Cold had all his savages on point but everybody was still chilling smoking and drinking but they still had there eye's on the prize.

All the Latin King's was waiting on the phone call to make it rain in some apartments so when the phone call came they headed to Washington Height's with murder on there mind. It only took the Latin Kings 20 minutes to pull inside Washington Height's, When they pulled in everything looked dead so they rode all the way in the back and killed there light's When the Latin King's pulled up they never seen the 4 killers standing in the cut behind the building. Inside the car the Latin Kings was inside getting there choppers together when they seen a group of people running towards them shooting bullet after bullet. The first set of bullets hit the car, And that made the Latin King's try to make a run for it; but the first person to get hit was the driver and he got hit in the neck wit a chopper. The other two made the worst move of there life when they looked down at there falling comrade. When they looked up they was looking down the barrel of 8 choppers with bullets coming out of them. When the smoke cleared all the Latin Kings was laying dead half way outside there car... Miguel just sat back and wondered why every time he order a hit nothing seem to go right. So Miguel picked up his phone and called Roc two times after the third try Miguel threw his phone against his office wall; and fired up a Cuban cigar and sat in his chair and tried to come up with a master plan...... After a long night of restless sleep Miguel woke up to the sun in his eye's and his house phone ringing, After 15 minutes of the same caller calling Miguel woke up to the voice of Cisco and the first words he heard was. We need to fall back off of these mission's because they waiting on us to come!! said Cisco into the phone. Look I still want everything to go as planned! Ya'll just need to do it better next time! That's what ya'll get paid for!! Now get off this phone and get to work!! said Miguel hanging up his house phone and he knew he had to up his game with Freeze, Slim and Bat Man or his time was coming up next. The look on Cisco face was straight destruction he just sat and looked at the map on the wall and knew that every place Miguel sent them was death traps and he had to follow suit because Miguel was in the seat. So Cisco dialed the number for the next group of workers to make there worst move ever.

Slim had already put everybody on high watch so the first person to move was Big Jitt; he had everybody on point from the front to the back to the sides, he made sure every gun man was on point and every trap had work before he left for the night. Once everything was done Big Jitt pulled off.

The whole ride the Latin Kings was just thinking because they knew this hit was a death trap but they knew if they didn't do the job they was dead. So they just rode in silence known they only had seconds to live... All Big Jitt soulja's was on post and everybody had high powered rifle's and all of them had a hundred round drum's and everybody was on point until all Jitt soulja's was ready to shoot any car pulled in, then they seen a car pull in and they just watched them roll it but they followed them until they hit the corner, But when the other soulja's seen the car they unloaded on sight.

When the three Latin King's drove pass the apartment complex everything was looking like a ghost town so the driver thought it was safe for them to take a look around; Because if anybody would've seen on first look they would've thought the driver was the only one inside so he drove around but before he hit the bin the whole section lit up with gun fire... When Big Jitt soulja's finished with the Latin king's car it looked like the car off of set it off.

Word moved around fast about the Latin King's trying to hit all of Freeze, Slim and Bat Man apartment's and trap houses that they felt they needed to start watching all the Latin King traps and safe houses but they knew they had a lot of work to do because they knew all the Latin King spot's was gimmie's so Slim and Bat Man sat at the chess board and came up with a fool proof plan. While Freeze sat there and watched the game and listened to the plan. Slim was the white pieces so he made his move and started the conversation... I feel like we need to start watching all and every Latin mother fucker in Duval county! said Slim looking at the chess board. Even tho they making some fucked up moves! It's a reason why they making all these fucked up moves! So I feel we really need to watch every one of them before we make a move because something or somebody ain't right and we need to find out what the play is with these bitches!! said Slim looking at Bat Man and Freeze. Bat Man made his move and said check! Slim just looked at the board because he didn't see that move coming. And he knew it was check mate in the next two moves. So Slim knocked over his king and looked at Bat Man. When Slim looked at Bat Man; Bat Man looked at Freeze then Freeze looked at both of them and stood up. Me and Bat Man will work this! But we still need to have a meeting to put everybody on point! said Freeze still standing but looking into space. Ok I'll do that now! And I want ya'll to chill until after the meeting! said Slim picked up his phone and called everybody; and everybody was there with in 45 minutes talking and ready to make that next power move. But all the main people was talking before Slim, Freeze or Bat Man walked out the house.

About 1 hour after everybody pulled-up Slim had Freeze and Bat man in the room facing where everybody was; talking about everything

Freezing in Duval

that couldn't be said around everybody... "look ya'll: before we walk out there!! I need to tell ya'll this!! I feel like something or somebody ain't right!! said Slim, And with that being said they walked out the door, and everybody stopped what they was doing and looked at Slim, Freeze, and Bat man walk out. When they walked up Slim walked through two chairs while Freeze and Bat man sat down and watched movements and faces, while Slim held the floor.

"Look" We asked everybody together because this shit looking crazy for us right now!! Something looking fucked up!! said Slim while he looked at everybody faces. And we hope there's nobody in this circle!! Slim stopped again and looked at everybody in the yard except the two on the patio with him.

Once he checked every face in front of him he finished. Because shit going to get real ugly!! "Now" with this war!! It's looking good!! But ya'll don't get to loose, and lose your head!! said Slim walking around talking. So everybody head back to there spots and make sure all your workers is on post 24-7!! Because we never know when they going to make a good move!! So we need to always stay on point!! said Slim watching every face in the yard.

After Slim said that he turned around and followed Freeze and Bat man in the house.

After everybody left Slim sat at the chess board about to play his self when Freeze walked up and sat in front of him and pushed his King Side Pawn up two spots, and looked at Slim.

Then Slim pushed his King Side Pawn up two and looked at Freeze. I'm glad to see you back! said Slim with a slit smile on his face. Freeze just looked and moved his Queen Side Knight.

So what's the plan on the watch? Slim moved his Queen Side Pawn then looked at Freeze. "Bruh" You already know!! we don't need no play book!! we just play "Freeze stood up and flipped one of his rooks over and turned to leave out the door; but before he hit the door he turned around and faced Slim to leave him with a thought. And we always win!! said Freeze walking out the room.

Freeze turned and walked out the door and sat on the passenger side and looked at Bat man. It's fair game whatever we find we keep!!

said Freeze still looking at Bat Man. Bat man just turned his head and pulled off headed to the west side to do there homework on the Bosses.

Miguel sat around thinking about all the wrong information he received from his source and was wondering why everything was turning on him, So he grabbed his gun and his hat and headed to straighten the mess he was making It was going on two weeks of watching the same thing, That Freeze changed the whole set-up.

The first day of watching the club everything was packed and moving fast so they barely seen anything. Now on the second and third things was slowing down but you couldn't put faces with names, Freeze and Bat Man had hundreds of pictures of different people and different Bosses of the Latin Kings. So they made mental notes that the next person they torture, They put the names to the faces.

Things was looking better on the fourth and fifth day. Things slowed down and more people slide through the spot's, But one of the faces almost killed Freeze, Someone that he looked up to his whole life was with the enemy, and he knew he had to be the one to kill him.

Bat man looked at Freeze and shook his head because he knew what the out come was going to be, so they sat outside in silence until they seen Suicide walk out and pull off, Then they pulled off behind him.

After Freeze followed Suicide for about three hours and seen all the family stops. He turned off and headed to the safe house. Shit was getting to the point where Suicide just wanted to call and tell Freeze, Slim and Bat man what's been going on, but he knew that was a funny game to play with his life. So things had to be how they was until he made his next move, if he had time to.

Bat man had already made the call to Slim, So when they pulled up all the lights was on and the front door was unlocked. Freeze pulled in like a bolt of lighting and walked through the door in mid sentence. Bruh I can't believe this fuck ass shit!!! said Freeze mad. Guess what we just seen at this fuck ass club!! Before Slim could speak Freeze was back at it. We seen this creep ass nigga Suicide walking in this bitch acting like everything was sweet!! Slim dropped his cup, turned around and walked in the game room and sat at the chess board. Because he didn't know how much Suicide had told them; So the whole game had done flipped for the worst.

So everybody just sat in there on zone thinking how fucked up the game was and how everybody in their family was sour. The only people they could trust was themselves, and the people in there room, And they knew it was some fuck niggaz in their circle but they didn't know who to trust right now, So first they had to get everything Suicide knew and fast. So they sat and thought about there next move until they fell asleep in the game room.

The next morning all three of them got up with one thing on their mind and that was Suicide, and trying to find out the best way to do there job. Because they knew Suicide was a killer from the old school and they knew they had to play their cards to the fullest, So Slim and Bat man sat back and waited on Freeze to make the call because everything on this hit, was his call.

After about 30 minutes Freeze stoop up with his plan. Look on some real gangsta shit!! We going to play this as cut throat as they playing it!! said Freeze with a look of straight hate.

I'm going to wait for his birthday! Then I'm going to blow his mother fucking brains out!! Slim and Bat man stood up; walked over to Freeze and dapped him up. And they all walked in the kitchen looking for something to eat.

When Miguel pulled up everybody was inside the house but five Kings was on the porch with choppers, So Miguel walked pass them and walked in the house and seen Kings everywhere with Lady Kings walking around half naked. When they seen him everybody kept doing what they was doing like he had no rank, When Miguel seen that it made him so mad he walked to the radio and slammed it on the ground and walked in the back room where he knew Roc or Cisco or both was back there.

When Miguel walked in he seen a Lady King on her knees in front of Roc, when he turned his head he seen Cisco with a Lady King bent over hitting her from the back, Miguel just rolled his eyes and walked back out the door and closed it and gave them 5 minutes to get right and knocked back on the door and walked in and seen them doing the same thing but he started talking to them while they was still busy.

"Look" I don't understand why ya'll disrespect me like ya'll do!! said Miguel looking at Cisco and Roc. Or not doing what I asked!!! But as of tonight something have to give!! Ya'll need to tell me something!! Because I really feel like ya'll think I'm a bitch or something!! said Miguel getting madder as he talked.

So what's the play!! Because ya'll don't want me to go off my own thought!!! said Miguel walking closer. When Cisco heard that he pulled out and pulled up his pants and went off on Miguel. You is a real mother fucking bitch!! said Cisco moving closer to Miguel. And I don't appreciate the way you brung your soft ass in here trying to act like you the one pay me!! so you better find somebody else to play with before you get your mother fucking head bust wide open!! said Cisco looking at Miguel waiting on him to say anything or bust a move. But before Miguel could say anything Roc had got dressed and was telling him how he felt. "That's some real g-shit bruh just told you!!

The only reason we haven't killed your bitch ass yet is because of my brother!! But you is walking on very thin ice!! So if I was you I'll just leave and go home before your bitch ass come up missing!! said Roc looking Miguel in his eye's.

As Miguel stood there all the workers and members was walking up listening to Roc & Cisco, So when Roc finished talking Miguel looked around and seen that the odds was against him so he held his words and walked to the car and pulled off.

The whole ride Miguel was just thinking how he just got tried like he was a bitch and how everybody over there was against him, an he knew it was time for him to get some help before he whined up in a ditch!! So the whole ride he was thinking of every kind of way to handle it without the head Kings stepping in so he just rode the rest of the way trying to figure it out. So he pulled over at a gas station and called the only person that would help him right now and didn't judge him.

On the third ring he heard the voice of Juan... "Hello" this better be good Miguel.

Miguel took a deep breath and told Juan the play.

"Ok look" I'm trying to do my part on this war!! but I'm not getting no help from our team!! I just went over there and tried to talk to them and they just laughed!! So I went to talk to "Roc and Cisco" and they just straight up told me in my face they'll kill me if I say anything else to them!! So what I'm suppose to do about this? asked Miguel confused.

The whole time Miguel was talking, Juan was thinking and he knew what they was doing. All the workers and the members knew that Miguel didn't know how to call shots so Juan just waited until he finished and told him how to handle that. "Ok" I understand what you saying!! but the only thing you can do is fall back and chill! "Now" you just lay back and chill and let me talk to them!! said Juan.

Miguel face was fire red when he didn't hear nothing he wanted to hear. So he just calmed down and ended the conversation, looked at his phone and threw it out the window and pulled off Known he was on a solo mission.

Freeze and Bat man was on full watch on Suicide, everything he did they knew about it, they even had workers watching his house when he went in for the night. Freeze made sure he had Suicide every move, Suicide was the one showed him the game and besides that he was his uncle. And he stayed on point that's why him slipping threw him off so much. Because that's one thing he barely did, so that made Freeze think it was a set-up, but how everything was looking, it still show that he was sour as fuck so that made everyday better for freeze, But this game of chess was for keeps, So he was always 8 moves ahead of him, and Freeze knew he couldn't play him like they did the Kings. So he stayed on point at all times.

The whole time Suicide never knew he had so many eyes on him from sun up to sun down, that was a flaw Suicide had build, he got to relaxed in the game and that was about to cost him his life soon... While Freeze and Bat man was on post, Slim was making sure everything was going the way it supposed to go, He had major eyes on all the spots the Kings was running on the low and they had black people running trying to throw them off, Until he seen two of the faces that was on the pictures walking in the after hour spots, When Slim remembered the faces he went to the other after hour spot and seen two more of the Kings walking in the back door, So for the next whole week Slim watched both of the spots and every cut and corner, after Slim felt he had all the work done he went back to his house to give what he seen some thought.

Things was looking real crazy for Haviar in the street, things haven't came down on him yet because the other Bosses knew he could hold his on in the streets so they stayed out all the street business, and let him handle it, but Haviar still felt he needed to put Juan on the front line again, but he was going to wait for a month before he put Juan back in his spot. Just to see if Miguel could handle his business.

Juan waited two days before he called Roc, on the first ring Juan heard Roc voice… "What's up bruh"!! How you feeling? I'm feeling much better I'm ready to kill these mother fuckers!! said Juan into the phone. I feel ya bruh!! But what's up with the call!! said Roc confused. "O" I got a job I need ya'll to do!! It's some apartments on Davis St called Blodgett Homes!! I need ya'll to go through there and kill everything moving!! said Juan. That's what's up!! We on that ASAP bruh you just take it easy until you come back!! said Roc. and anyway!! When is you coming back? The way everything looking, real soon!! Ya'll just make that happen for me and I'll feel much better!! said Juan hanging up his phone with a smile on his face.

After Roc hung up the phone he looked and Cisco, from the look Roc gave Cisco, he knew that was Juan with something to do so Cisco just sat there and let Roc give him the run down. "Ok" we got action!! That was bruh telling us he want everything dead in the Blodgett Homes!! ASAP!! said Roc looking at Cisco. That's what's up so we really only need choppers and extra clips!! said Cisco grabbing his tool for work. That's all!! Let's go it's still early so people everywhere right now… said Roc walking out the door behind Cisco. In the Blodgett Homes people was on their porch drinking while other people was walking around, while a couple of Slim, Freeze and Bat man workers was rotating around making plays, while the children ran around.

After about two hours of everybody chilling, the whole sky looked liked it opened. Rain was falling and people was running for cover, while the people on their porch walked in their house and closed their door; while the workers and a few flip-flop-poppers stood up under the mail box talking.

When Roc got off the interstate the rain started coming down hard, so they still rode down Davis st into the Apartments. When they first rode in, they didn't see nobody, so Roc turned around to drive in the back when they seen three jitts with all black on and two females standing under the mailbox. When Roc and Cisco seen that, Cisco loaded his and Roc chopper, And Roc whipped the car to the curve and grabbed his chopper, And him and Cisco jumped out. Two of the workers was talking to the flip-flop-poppers.

While the other worker was texting on the phone, nobody seen the car pull up, or the two Latino men jump out with the choppers until bullets started coming from everywhere. The first set of bullets hit the worker who was texting and both of the flip pop poppers. The other two workers tried to run but Roc and Cisco changed clips and chopped both of the workers up. Once Roc and Cisco seen everybody was dead they ran to there car and pulled off while the old people called Slim or Bat man or Freeze.

All the phones was ringing but the only one answered was Slim... after Slim got all the phone calls from the different people, he sat back and just thought about what he just heard, so that let him know they was falling in his trap every new spot he opened they was going for them so Slim figured that he'll put a few more niggaz on the chopping block while he came up with a master plan to end this war because Slim was getting to the point that the game was getting old to him, so he was making plans to get out. But after he made sure everything was good on his end. So Slim just laid back down next to Monay and kissed her on her forehead, while he thought about his next move because Freeze and Bat man was watching Suicide, so everything was on him.

The next morning Slim woke up to breakfast in bed and Monay in an apron naked walking out the room door looking back. Once Slim finished his pancakes, beef links and eggs, he started his day making phone calls to people that he needed to put in work, the first person he called was Rosco. When Rosco answered Slim gave him the run down fast.

It's a after hour spot on the east side that some niggaz run!! But them Latin Kings own it!! So I need you to just ride by there and make sure they know it's us passing by... said Slim closing his phone. When Slim dropped the phone Monay started crawling on the bed. So Slim moved the sheets so Monay could see his wood, When Monay seen that her mouth got watery so she slide her mouth on Slim manhood until he stopped her and rolled her over and slide his manhood inside of Monay. After about 40 minutes Slim and Monay was back in the bed sleep.

The address Slim gave Rosco led him to the 16th and Phoenix block, when Rosco pulled up he seen a line of people, his first mind told him to just shoot the people in line, but he parked his car and walked to the door and asked the doorman what's the closing time so when the doorman told him 6 o'clock, Rosco walked back to his car and looked at his watch and seen he had three more hours before the club closed. So after Rosco made sure that his chopper was good and he had two hundred round clips taped together. Once everything was good Rosco sat and waited on the club to end.

Inside the joint was packed, people was from wall to wall dancing and talking when they heard the DJ say last drink, most of the people left, but the true party animals stayed until the light's came on, when they did everybody was on their way out the door when they heard gun shots. When Rosco looked at his watch it said 5:45 so he grabbed his old faithful chopper and walked towards the front door You had people walking out talking while other people stood and watched the cars pass by. Nobody seen Rosco walk in front of the club and open up until it was to late. People was falling from everywhere, people heads was hitting their horns while other people was trying to run and live. But when Rosco flipped his clip he went ham. Rosco started walking up on everybody he seen moving on the ground putting bullets in the back or the front of their heads.

After Rosco finished there where 17 men and 12 women, three club workers and 1 bartender dead in the streets. When Slim got the news he called Baldy and had him check out the other after hour spot the Kings had on the West Side, Slim knew he was winning this game playing four moves ahead.

When Baldy got the info he was already on the West Side the only thing he had to do was show up and make shit happen.

At the spot people was standing more outside then on the inside so the DJ moved all his music equipment to the outside and everybody that was in the inside moved outside. The old cat that was looking over the spot made a drink special for all the ladies, two for one, so all the ladies had two or four cups on their table, and the men was walking around trying to get the females to get their drinks for them. But everything was moving smooth at the spot and people was pulling up by the minute.

The whole time people was walking and standing in the yard, nobody seen Baldy posted up in the bushes across the street. Havair was fire hot when he got word that his after hour spot on the east side got hit last night. But when he got the video from the outside he seen it was a massacre, the only thing he could do was sit back and try to figure out his next move, But his only thought keep going to calling a small meeting with the five heads of the Latin Kings. So with no more thought Havair made the phone calls and set the date for the meeting. After all the calls was made Havair sat back in his love seat and fired up a Cuban cigar and shook his head because he knew things was getting ugly for them and desperate times brings desperate measures so he pulled a card that he shouldn't have pulled but he knew the Bosses will have his head, because they didn't know about the after hour spots he had going.

So Havair just sat in his love seat and smoked his cigar until he fell asleep.

Baldy just sat and watched everybody movements and waited until everybody started feeling there self then he checked his Mac 90 and made his move on the crowd... Nobody knew what hit them when Baldy jumped out the bushes spraying his Mac. People tried to run and hide but Baldy was thrown his Mac like a real pro. When Baldy finished 22 Latin King member's 13 men and 9 females went to meet there maker On the ride to the meeting Havair got the phone call about the other after hour spot that got hit, So his mind went straight to how the other bosses was going to take his little extra side money. But he knew he had to put them up on game, Because things was looking to crazy for him to keep any secret's; and he knew they was going to find out about his extra money inside the spot. When Havair pulled in he seen everybody car so he knew everybody was waiting on him so that made Havair move a little bit faster towards the door. When Havair grabbed the door knob the door was cracked so he walked in and the first person he seen was Sunny. Once Havair greeted Sunny he walked over to Sebastian and greeted him. (Now they was like one person anytime the Head Latin King bosses needed a big job done they would call them) Once Havair greeted Sunny and Sebastian he walked over and greeted the voice of the family Jesus then he looked over and nodded his head at Jesus two hit men; Pedro and Enrique. They hit men but they also bosses they just like to play the field. After Havair greeted everybody he started the meeting; Sorry for calling this meeting on short notice! But this shouldn't take to long! said Havair walking around talking. This war that we got going on is getting to serious!! They went to our after hour spot's and killed random people! said Havair looking every boss in there eye's. So that let me know they know who we is so we need to be careful! So in the mean time ya'll take a chill pill and I'll handle everything! said Havair hoping he had made his point. All the other bosses was looking at Havair like he was crazy but all of them agreed because they already knew that Havair was going to straighten them for there lost. When Havair seen that he ended the meeting and everybody went there separate ways going to finish off the rest of there night's while Havair rode feeling like he got across to his fellow King's..... Freeze and Bat Man pulled up at Slim house bright and early the next morning with a bag filled with picture's they took. And they came up with a plan to start knocking off everybody that be around Suicide because his birthday was coming up real soon and they had to move fast; real fast When they walked in they seen Slim sitting at the table with two extra plates and Monay was at the stove cooking breakfast. Bat Man walked in the dinning room dapped Slim and spoke to Monay and sat at the table across from Slim. While Freeze walked in the game room and 5 minutes later came right back out walked up behind Slim and tapped him on the back of the head then he walked up to Monay gave her a hug and a kiss on the check grabbed a beef link and sat at the table and listened to what Bat Man was already telling Slim about the next move. So like I was saying! We brung some picture's we took of some people, we seen with Suicide and them Latin King's!! said Bat Man looking at Slim smiling. Slim was sitting there loving the plan but he wanted Bat Man to get to the point. Because we going to knock off every Latin King we seen with him! Because if they with him they must be real important! said Bat Man looking Slim in his eye's smiling. When Bat Man said that Monay was bringing them there plates and juice. Once Monay fed everybody she walked in the back bedroom. After Slim, Freeze and Bat Man finished eating they walked in the game room. And Freeze walked straight to the bar and dumped the bag of pictures, while Slim walked over to the safe and grabbed the pictures he had and walked over to the bar and started handing them to Freeze and out of 12 picture's 5 of them matched the four pictures of the bosses Freeze had they was pictures of Sunny, Sebastian, Enrique, Pedro and Jesus. Freeze looked at the pictures and passed them to Bat Man and Bat Man passed them to Slim and in every picture Suicide was either dapping or hugging a Latin King boss and in every picture Suicide was smiling. Slim threw the pictures on the bar and looked at Freeze with straight hate in his eye's. I'm going on a couple of these!! said Slim looking at Freeze and Bat Man. Freeze just looked at Slim and started packing the pictures. That's what up bruh!! It's just us everybody else on close watch!! said Freeze walking out with Bat Man on his heels going to handle there job watching Suicide. While Slim went to work on the bosses... Bat Man worked night and day watching Suicide waiting on one of the bosses to pull up. But it was late one night when Bat Man was on watch he seen a Black Expedition pull into Suicide driveway and one of the Latin King bosses got out and Suicide greeted him at the door with a hug and they walked inside the house... When Bat Man seen that he woke Freeze up. Bruh! Bruh! said Bat Man trying to wake Freeze up. Before Bat Man could say his name again Freeze woke up grabbing his 40 Cal looking for anything to kill until he heard Bat Man telling him that one of the Latin King bosses just walked inside Suicide house. When Freeze heard that he went to full focus. What you said bruh? said Freeze looking at Suicide house. Bat Man just went to the bag and pulled out the picture of who he just seen walk inside Suicide house. When Freeze seen the picture he could only think of Baby face. O!! So he just went in there? said Freeze with murder in his eye's. Yep that was him! said Bat Man ready for the move. That's what's up! We going to sit and chill and wait on him to come out and do our thang!! said Freeze still looking at Suicide house. It was almost 4 hours before they seen Suicide and the Latin King boss walk on the porch talking. When Bat Man seen that he pulled off headed for the main rode waiting on the boss to pull out. 15 minutes after Bat Man pulled up across the street the boss was pulling out of Suicide driveway and Bat Man pulled right behind him... Inside the car Sebastian was on the phone telling Sunny the whole talk he had with Suicide. Well just like I said Bruh! He said we can get bricks for 25 thou!! said Sebastian into the phone. So he said we can get them for 25? said Sunny happy into the phone. Then he said whatever we buy he'll throw us! So how many you told him we going to get? said Sunny happy. I told him we was going to get 10 of them things! said Sebastian getting happy as he talked. So that make 20!! When we going to get them bruh? said Sunny. Probably in two we...... Bat Man was driving behind the S.U.V when he just ran straight in the back of it when they was getting off the interstate in Lake Forest Sebastian was in mid sentence when a car ran into the back of them. Sebastian and the driver was so mad that they was trying to jump out the S.U.V. But Bat Man and Freeze was already outside the car with straight murder on there mind. Bat Man walked up on the driver and shot him 6 times in the body then unloaded the rest of his clip in his face then turned around to watch Freeze. When Sebastian seen his driver getting killed he reached for his gun but Freeze was already on the side of him and unloaded his 40 Cal in the side of his face after he made sure he was dead he jumped in the car and him and Bat Man rode down Edge wood Sunny was on the other end listening to his brother lose his life, And the only thought ran threw his mind was murder and pay back As Bat Man drove Freeze was on the passenger side doing something. So Bat Man looked in Freeze hand and seen him playing with a cell phone. Nigga where you got that from! asked Bat Man looking at Freeze. Shit!! Off tha Chico back there! He was on here talking to somebody named Sunny! said Freeze looking at Bat Man. But I see some pictures in this phone that I recognize; so we need to slide threw some of these places and see what we see After Freeze gave Bat Man the direction's Bat Man rode up on a house and they seen one of the men on the picture standing on the porch kissing his wife so Freeze grabbed his 223. with the hundred round drum and gave the order. Block the driveway Bruh!! said Freeze looking at the car pulling out the driveway; but right before the car hit the street Bat Man pulled up and Freeze jumped out and unloaded his 223. in the driver side window and door; when Freeze finished you could see blood dripping through the door Bat Man seen the boss wife running towards the car; as soon as she hit the back of the car Bat Man hit her three times in the chest and they pulled off headed for the safe house Havair got the news about Sebastian, Sunny and his wife and almost cried. Because he knew it was time to put Juan back over the street because they was losing real bad in this war they was in and he knew he had to gain control over it real soon before things got any worst for them. So Havair walked out his house headed for Juan house. When Havair pulled up he seen Juan watering his grass so he jumped out and walked up to Juan. When he seen Havair he knew it had to be something serious because he don't do house calls. So Juan walked over and turned his water off and sat on the porch and waited for Havair to come join him. As soon as Havair sat down he got straight to the point. Look I need you back on post asap!! said Havair looking Juan in his eye's. I been ready! What happened? asked Juan ready to get back in his seat. Boy!! That damn Slim, Freeze and that damn Bat Man killed Sebastian, Sunny and his wife!! said Havair making a cross on his chest. When Juan heard that a tear rolled down his face. When Havair seen that he added the rest. Now we need to at least know how they look! said Havair looking Juan in the eye's. Juan just looked back at Havair and stood up. I know how Slim look! But trying to find all three of them together is going to be hard! But with the information I got from Brother Mark we'll just knock off them other apartments they got and stop there money! Then we'll knock them off! said Juan looking at Havair. Havair just looked back at Juan hoping that his word was gold; when Juan finished talking Havair stood up. I hope everything you say is gold! I'm going to give you a year to clean up this none sense!! said Havair looking at Juan serious. Juan just stood there listening until Havair was done and he said the worst thing he could've ever said. Juan raised up his hand and when they shook Juan looked Havair in the eye's. I'll have this done in 8 month's don't worry yourself. And with that being said Juan walked back over and finished watering his grass. When Juan finished watering his grass he walked in the house and made his phone calls. On the first ring Roc answered the but the back ground was loud because Roc was giving all the little King order's. When Roc finished talking to all the little King's Juan started giving him the run down. Look Havair just put me back on the seat! And he gave us 8 month's to end this war we got going on! So I need ya'll to make a move on all there spot's! Safe houses! And Trap"s!! Asap!! said Juan feeling good that he was back in power. We don't have know time to waste! said Juan hanging up his phone... When Juan hung up he felt the power but one thing he didn't know was all power come to a end.

When Freeze pulled up Bat man was in the back seat sleep but when he felt the car turn off he jumped up and followed Freeze in the house. When they walked in they didn't see Slim so they walked to the back and seen him sitting on the back porch smoking a jay. So Freeze and Bat man walked up and sat beside him. After two more pulls Slim passed the jay and told them what was on his mind. "Hey ya'll" I been out here thinking about all the hits, And Baldy and Trav be half doing their jobs!! Freeze just looked at Slim and didn't understand what he was talking about until Slim laid it flat out for them. What I'm saying is!! They use all them bullets and only kill two dam people!! said Slim laughing. Freeze and Bat man busted out laughing because they knew they killed more people then that but Slim was feeling some type of way so they just sat back and listened to him.

So ya'll know a lot of the workers trying to move up! So after we handle all this shit we in; I'll have somebody start looking!! Why you say that bruh? said Bat Man looking confused. Because a lot of our workers about to die!! "So" I'm just saying for the future!! said Slim looking at

Freeze and Bat Man. Freeze and Bat man almost forgot what they came over there for. Freeze had to tell Slim what was going on. Bruh I got some fuck shit going on!! Well we do!! We invested our money in some shit Suicide had going on!! Slim dropped his head. Then when Freeze told him how much it was Slim almost fell out. How much ya'll gave him again?

We gave him $750,000 a piece!! Dam ya'll know that's a lost right? said Slim. Both Freeze and Bat man sat down with their head down because they knew the only thing they had left was their guns and the money that was in the streets.

Roc & Cisco sat in the house trying to figure out what was the best move for them and the apartments hits. Roc & Cisco did their homework on the apartments they learned every hole in the fence and all but the worst thing was it was one way in one way out, Cisco knew some females that chilled out there that was going to call them when any of Slim workers showed up.

It took almost a week to get the phone call about a cook-out Slim workers was having, so Roc and Cisco called up a few workers and gave them the hit for tonight. Inside Cleveland arms apartments It was live as fuck in there; One of the real nigga's from the apartments just came home from prison, So everybody showed up to show their love and suppose for a real nigga. Slim sat back thinking about the cook-out and if anything went wrong at this function, they had to move their family into a safe place then they'll know that Suicide was working with the enemy.

Slim had a Big Bash planned for almost a year; So everybody was ready when the day came, Slim had Jenkins and Holly's Bar-b-que to come out and cater to the celebration of a real street nigga touching down. When you pulled in you had people setting up tents for one of he local Djs, DJ Nu-sht. After the sun fell, cars started to pull up from everywhere and every side of town, females pulled out their Sunday's best to show their face on the scene. When Nu-Sht turned up the ones and twos everybody started walking around vibeing and dancing; Some people was at the open bar getting their drink on, When the show of the party pulled up in a stretch hummer with four bad bitches with him two on each side of his arm's. They walked over to the area they had set-up for him in the corner behind the DJ booth.

When the new members got the call for the hit, they was already close to the apartments and they knew the area good so they drove around the back of the apartments and loaded up their choppers and jumped out of the splack and ran for the wholes that was in the back of the apartments' fences.

It was four hours since everybody showed up and everybody was feeling themselves, people had started walking to their cars while other people stood around talking and smoking. Nobody knew what hit them when the three Kings came blasting around the corner, shooting any and everybody in sight, the three King ran in through three different holes in the fence so when they ran in they covered more ground, people was trying to shoot back but it was no good when the Kings finished it was 15 men shot, 15 workers dead, and 20 women that was shot and killed. News had spread so fast about the hit that when Haviar received the news he was happy but he knew they had a lot more work to do in the near future and he was happy about the progress, but he knew Slim had a trick up his sleeve, but he didn't know how far Slim would go. So he knew how the game was looking for now on, Because he knew Slim wouldn't slip like that twice.

Slim sat back thinking about the hit and how everything went and the only thing he could do was shake his head and laugh, Because he knew they had to move their families again, But as he thought; he was the only person with a family. And Monay was pregnant with twins and she was due in four more weeks, So Slim just sat in his office thinking until Monay walked in. and before she could say a word Slim had her to come sit on his lap.

When Monay sat down Slim rubbed her stomach and kissed her on the lips. When that happened Monay knew something wasn't right so she stood up and walked over to the back and fixed Slim a drink and walked it back over to him, then she walked over to Slim desk and opened the top drawer and pulled out some already grinned loud and a white owl and rolled a blunt for Slim and a paper jay for herself. Then she fired up Slim blunt an passed it to him then she sat back on Slim lap and fired up hers, Then after they smoked Monay broke the silence. So baby is you going to tell me what's wrong with you? said Monay looking Slim in the eye's standing up. Slim just sat there in another world until he stood up about to walk out the room not realizing Monay was talking. So is you going to tell me or what? said Monay while Slim walked. When Slim heard that he stopped walking and start giving Monay the run down on what was going on. I know how you be saying you don't want to move from this house! said Slim turning around to look at Monay. Yeah I be saying that but get to the point! said Monay sitting down to face Slim. Slim knew he had to sit next to Monay because she looked at Mark as a father figure and Suicide like a uncle and he knew it was going to hurt her to know that Mark and Suicide was working with the Latin King's. So Slim walked over to a empty chair and pulled it next to Monay an sat down with his mind still wondering about how Mark and Suicide was out to kill him Freeze and Bat Man, So Slim downed his drink and let it flow out the only way he knew how. (And that was real nigga talk). Bae Mark and Suicide working with the Latin King's trying to kill me Freeze and Bat Man! When Slim said that Monay whole face went pale, Slim had to catch her from falling out the chair and carry her to the sofa and made a fan out of some paper and fanned her until she cooled off then Slim walked in the guess room and grabbed a fan and pointed it at her on low with a glass of warm water. About 25 to 30 minutes later Monay sat up and Slim finished the story. After Slim finished telling her some of the fact he sat next to her and asked her which one of the other houses she wanted to move into. Monay just sat there thinking for about 30 minutes before she said North Carolina. Slim just stood there and smiled and told her to pack her bag's then Slim walked in the game room and opened the closet and moved the knight on the chess board he had set up and that move was check mate on Brother Mark. So Slim spun the board and set the pieces back up now this time he was white and Mark was black. After Slim made his move he slid the chess board back in the closet and walked over to the window and thought just how sour the people was who raised them; and how he couldn't wait until Mark crossed that line, And how much he really didn't want to wait he had to so he just waited until Freeze and Bat Man came through so he could give them the next move.

The Head Latin King bosses was thinking it was Brother Mark or Suicide that put Slim, Freeze and Bat Man on there trail that cost Sunny and his wife and Sebastian there life so they called a sit down with Brother Mark and Suicide to see how they handle pressure. At the sit down Jesus and his henchmen and Brother Mark and Suicide and there henchmen sat at the table while Jesus talked about what was going on and how he felt about the problem. But like I'm saying me or Brother Mark don't have nothing to lie about! Ya'll need our help with them! They don't need our help with ya'll!! said Suicide looking Jesus in his eye's. Jesus face was fire red from anger, Before Jesus spoke he picked up a phone and mashed a button and the whole room was filled with Latin King's with all types of big gun's. Before Suicide or Brother Mark people could make a move the Latin King's was taking there weapon's. Suicide tried to talk but was stopped mid sentence. Look before ya'll leave here tonight one for ya'll is going to tell me where Slim, Freeze or that nigga Bat Man live! said Jesus looking at Suicide. Suicide looked at Brother Mark and seen a tear rolling down his face. Brother Mark knew that his life was on the line either way and he knew this was the beginning to his end; so after Mark cried for a few more minutes he pulled out his phone and texted Jesus Slim address and looked at Suicide and dropped his head. When Jesus got the text he stood up and him and his henchmen walked out while the other Latin Kings unclipped Suicide and Brother Mark henchmen gun's laid them on the table and walked out. The only thing Suicide and Brother Mark could do from that day on was pray. After Slim had some of there workers move him and Monay stuff, He called Rosco with the new order's. On the first ring Slim heard Rosco voice so Slim gave him the run down. Look I need you to send Trav and Cardo to my old house to look for anything that look funny! So you want them to move if they see anything? said Rosco confused. No!! I just need to know if anything going down! That's what's up I'm on it Bruh!! said Rosco hanging up his phone. Slim hung up his phone then walked to the car Monay was in and kissed her on the lips before the car pulled off. Slim stood there watching the car pull off and was happy

Freezing in Duval

that he stayed on point at all times. Freeze and Bat Man stayed posted on the block and on the front line. Every time trouble came they was right there, and there ear's was deep to the street's they was getting so much information that they was running out of bullet's. So one day one of Freeze and Bat Man workers pulled in the yard in a movers truck. When he jumped out Freeze and Bat Man had there guns pointed at his body. Nigga you almost got yourself killed with that bull shit; riding in that big ass truck! said Freeze laughing. There worker just stood there laughing until Freeze finished talking then he walked to the back of the truck and opened the door and Freeze and Bat Man mouth dropped from what they seen. On the inside was bullet's and guns of all type's while Freeze and Bat Man looked the worker gave them the run down. I felt like we was running low on gun's and ammo so I hit a train late last night and came up with this. The only thing Freeze and Bat Man could do was dap him up and tell him where to park the truck. Once the worker pulled off one of Bat Man people called him with some important information so Bat Man listened while Freeze watched. Once Bat Man got off the phone he gave Freeze the run down. One of my people I showed the pictures to just called me and told me one of the Head bosses named Enrique got a house in Plam Dale! said Bat Man looking at Freeze for the next play. Freeze just looked listening until a text message came in through Bat Man phone with the boss address to his house. See here's the address right here! said Bat Man handing Freeze the phone. Freeze looked at the phone and knew right where the house was. Ok we start looking asap! said Freeze walking towards the car while Bat Man walked behind him with murder in his eye's ready to go to work... Enrique was sitting in his living room watching T.V until his phone started ringing. Hello who this! said Enrique still looking at T.V. This Sosa! Remember you told me to come pick you up at 11:00!! said Sosa into the phone. When Enrique heard that he looked at his clock and seen it was 10:45. Damn! Where you at? said Enrique jumping out his chair. I'm turning on your street now! Ok!! Ride to the bar on Lem Turner and grab a bottle!! said Enrique trying to find something to put on. What bar the "Gate's"? said Sosa confused. Yeah and I'll be ready to go when you come back! When Enrique hung up his phone he found something to throw on and took a quick shower and got dressed... Outside the driver pulled back up in the driveway with the music blasting focused on texting his baby momma that he didn't even see Bat Man run up on the driver side until it was to late. Bat Man ran up on the driver side door hoping it was unlocked until he pulled the door open and had the driver outside dead with multiple stab wounds to his neck before he knew what hit him. When Freeze seen that him and Bat Man carried the driver body on the side of the house then Bat Man slide on the driver hat and got in the driver seat and Freeze got into the passenger seat and about 15 minutes later the boss came walking out of the front door. It was so dark outside that he couldn't see that it was two people in the front seat. So Enrique got in and gave the driver a piece of paper with a address on it and Bat Man closed the glass to separate them and pulled off... The whole ride Enrique didn't notice they was going in the opposite direction until it was to late. Bat Man turned off on a dirt road that made Enrique know it was something up so he went for the door but the doors had the child safety locks on them so Enrique looked around trying to find anything to use but there was nothing to use until Enrique remembered he grabbed his 12 inch knife and posted up for the door to open but he seen the sliding glass open. Bat Man and Freeze was posted already when the glass came down. When they seen Enrique facing the door Freeze and Bat Man unloaded there 40 Cal's with the 32 round clip's in the body of Enrique. After they made sure he was dead they rolled back up the window and dropped the limo back off to Enrique house. After whipping down the limo they switched cars and headed to Slim house.

    Jesus stayed up all night calling Enrique phone but it keep on going to the voicemail so the next morning Pedro picked up Jesus up and they rode to Enrique, When they pulled up they seen the limo. But when they walked up they seen little pile's of blood and they seen blood dripping from the door so that made them run to the door that's when they seen Enrique laying on the floor with bullet hole's all through his body they went looking for the driver but didn't see him until the went walking around the house and seen his feet sticking out. The only thing Jesus could do was cry, He couldn't holed it any longer and he knew this war had to stop and soon. And he was going to do anything in his power to make it stop.

When Freeze and Bat man walked in the house it looked like somebody just walked in and took everything they wanted and left. When they seen that Freeze and Bat Man pulled out there fire stick's and did a walk through of the house once they checked the whole house they walked in the game room and seen a note written in codes telling them where to meet up at so they closed and locked every window in the house then they seen the car ducked off in the cut and knew it was Trav and Cardo.... When Freeze and Bat Man pulled up they seen Slim walking around in the house through the window. But when they walked inside they didn't see Monay so they waited on Slim to finish his phone call so they could get the update. When Slim got off his phone he looked at Freeze and Bat Man. I think ya'll need to roll a blunt off this!! said Slim walking towards his chair. After Freeze and Bat Man finished rolling up the three blunts, They fired up and Slim started telling them about the feeling he was having. I been feeling that Suicide or Brother Mark! One of them done told them Latin King's where we at!! said Slim looking at Freeze and Bat Man. Freeze and Bat Man just looked because they knew they had to move fast on knocking them boy's off. So once Slim seen he had there attention he gave them the other news. So that's way I moved Monay because she pregnant with my twin boy's and I can't take know kind of chances!! said Slim pulling on his blunt. When Freeze and Bat Man heard twins then boy's they jumped up; run over and started messing with him. Until Slim stopped them and got back on track Now with that out the way we got to make this war disappear! And as soon as possible!! said Slim standing up. Now I've been doing some homework and I got some info on one of them Latin King bosses named Pedro! And I got a picture with him and two people and one of them we know!! said Slim reaching in his pocket for the picture and handed it to Freeze. Freeze grabbed the picture and passed it to Bat Man. Then Bat Man took one look at the picture and looked at Freeze. Ain't this the same person we did last night!! said Bat Man. Hell yeah! said Freeze looking at Slim. Slim grabbed the picture; with one ya'll got? said Slim looking at Freeze and Bat Man. Once Freeze pointed at the person Slim finished talking. O ok ya'll murked his brother Enrique last night! Now I got the address to there main house! said Slim pulling out a piece of paper passing it to Freeze. When Freeze seen it he passed it to Bat Man. When Bat Man seen the address he dug in his pocket and pulled out a piece of paper he had some address on; and when he looked at both of the address he seen they matched. Hey Freeze remember the information that Latin King gave us the other night! Well this is the same info on Slim paper! said Bat Man passing the paper around. Once they seen that everything matched they made there plan for the other Boss.

When Jesus and Pedro left the meeting the first person Jesus called was Havair to let him know what was going on… On the third ring Havair answered and just listened to the voice on the other end…. Hey I just left Enrique house and found him and Sosa dead in the front yard!! Now I don't know how we suppose to fix this problem! But this need to end very fast!! So I got some info on Slim I'm going to send you the address; So ya'll can make a move on him Freeze and Bat Man!! said Jesus. Havair was so happy from what he just heard that he couldn't even think; This was the first time they had anything on Slim in a few years, so he was ready to make that power call. Ok send me the info! I'll get on that as soon as possible!! said Havair hanging up his phone waiting on the text to come threw. So Havair fixed his self a drink and sat watching the phone until it light up; When it lit up the first thing he did was call Juan. And on the first ring Havair heard Juan back ground so he started talking. Look!! I got some real good information for you!! I'm about to send you Slim address! said Havair waiting on Juan to say something. When Juan heard that he almost jumped out his bed. Hold up!! So you mean to tell me you about to send me Slim address! said Juan sitting on the side of his bed. Yeah that's exactly what I said and I want them dead like yesterday! So get on the move!! said Havair hanging up his phone smiling forwarding Juan Slim address.

As soon as Juan hung up his phone Slim address popped up so Juan made all his phone calls to Roc and Cisco and all the hit men; Then he texted everybody Slim address. Once Juan made sure everything was done, He laid back down in his bed with a smile thinking that everything was almost to a head "But he didn't know that everything that shined wasn't gold".

Roc and Cisco was sitting in the back yard talking about all the hit's Slim, Freeze and Bat Man been ordering on them and there team. Cisco just walked around in a circle listening to what Roc had on his mind I just can't believe these nigga's giving us this much hell! Shit we was here first and we're not leaving! said Roc feeling his phone going off in his pant's pocket. When Roc seen it was one of the trap's he stopped talking and answered. Hello what's going on over there? said Roc wondering why he was calling. O nothing! I was calling to let you know. Before the worker could finish Roc could hear gun shot's on the other line and know talking The whole time the worker was on the phone Rosco was walking in the kitchen to buy the 8th he had asked the worker did they have, Once the worker gave Rosco a look over he laid his gun on the breakfast bar and sat at the table weighting the 8th. Rosco just looked around for anymore people then he seen a Latin King walking down the hallway on the phone so Rosco made his move when the worker at the table pulled out his scale. Rosco pulled out his Glock 9 and shot the worker that was walking down the hall 4 times in the body, then Rosco turned around to see the Latin King that was at the table with his gun in his hand. But before the worker could shoot the back door came open and Ice Cold put 7 bullet's in the worker body then he walked up to the worker and unloaded the other 25 bullet's he had in his face and neck. Once Ice Cold made sure him was dead he walked back to there stolen car and waited on Rosco with the car in gear.

When Ice Cold pulled off they didn't see the car pull off the same time they did Roc and Cisco had a chill house around the corner from where everything went down so they loaded up and waited on the corner. When Roc seen the car he followed them until they turned inside a local gas station and the driver ran in the store and the passenger switched seats Roc pulled on the side of the store and waited until he seen somebody running out When Rosco switched seats he seen a call pull in behind them so he started watching it but the tint on the window's was to dark he couldn't see a face or how many people was in it so he reloaded his gun and watched until he seen a jitt running out the store and both doors opened Cisco was debating on them running in the store until they seen somebody with a black tee shirt run out the store. And just like vet's they jumped out the car gun's blazing When the jit ran out the store he never seen the two killers until it was to late. Roc and Cisco was on there job Cisco was low and Roc was high both of them was shooting trying to get the best shot Ice Cold was inside looking at everything that was going outside. So Ice Cold mind went into overdrive and the first thing popped in his mind was the video tape; So Ice Cold whipped out his gun and ran to the clerk... Give me that Mother Fucking tape before I murk your ass!! said Ice Cold jumping over the counter. When the clerk seen the gun and the extra long clip he pissed on his self before he started walking to the video recorder, after he mashed ejected on all 8 of the recorders he placed all 8 of the tape's inside a bag and handed it to Ice Cold. Once Ice Cold made sure he had all the tapes he shot the clerk twice in the chest and ran out the other door When Ice Cold looked around the building he seen Rosco getting off but the Latin Kings was backing him up so Ice Cold did what any real nigga would've did in that spot; He came from around the corner bussing his 40 Cal, Ice Cold hit Roc and Cisco car so many time that they backed back inside there car and pulled off but Ice Cold still ran behind them bussing his fire When Ice Cold and Rosco finished they pulled off into traffic Rosco couldn't believe what had just went down that he ran a red light, and before he knew it he was rolling up on another one that he almost ran until Ice Cold snapped him out his daze. Bruh you need to snap out of that shit!! We got murder weapon's in this bitch and you want to run traffic light's!! said Ice Cold shacking his head. Rosco didn't realize what he was doing until Ice Cold said something. Dam bruh my bad I was in a real zone for real! said Rosco pulling off at the light. That's what's up lets slide threw the trap and see what's going on! said Ice Cold firing up a half of jay turning up his new urko baller C.D.

    Roc and Cisco was so mad at how everything played out that they rode through a neighborhood that Slim, Freeze and Bat Man operated and the first person they seen they blew his head off and drove off.

Freezing in Duval

When Slim got the news he just laughed because everything was turning up, and everybody on there team was stepping up there game. But he still had a funny feeling about Lil Boss, Trav and Baldy; now they was some stand up little cat's but the only thing Slim hated was half done work, But Slim knew they real test was coming soon.

Four month's had passed and Monay was due any day. So Slim left for a couple of weeks until she had the twin's... So on the streets Freeze and Bat Man handled everything from the work to the hit's, they had the movement going strong. They had started watching everybody even the Head King named Pedro; But getting him was going to be hard because he never left the house in least he was going on a hit; Every time they followed him he was going to kill somebody, and he did it so swift that they couldn't even get close to him so they finished hitting all the workers and members until they had a opening.

Juan was making moves all over town but didn't none of his moves mattered because every time he made a move they would make 4 and every move they made was costly to the family. And things was looking ugly by the day for the Latin King's and he knew they had to move fast.

In North Carolina Slim was walking around the room putting on gloves talking to Doctor's ready for his two little gangsta's to come in this cut throat world. Because he knew he had to teach them the right way and the wrong way in the game. Because whatever they was going to do in life they was going to be the best at it. After everything was set up in the room the Doctor walked in because Monay had dilated to the point, that the first baby was trying to come out. So the Doctor walked over and 10 minutes later he grabbed the first baby and pulled him out and handed him to his nurse then 4 seconds later Slim other son came into the world with his eye's closed until he heard Slim voice then both of the baby's started crying for there father. The whole time the twin's was gone Slim was trying to come up with the right name to give them but his mind was blank thinking about all the shit that was going on in the street's. So Slim looked over at Monay and seen her reading the Bible and that's when the thought popped in his head. Baby there name is going to be Kane and Able! said Slim looking for a sign but Monay looked over at Slim and smiled and finished reading the word After all the paperwork was signed Slim sat in the chair holding both of his son's thinking about the difference he was going to have to make for them if he wanted the best for them. But while Slim was in his thought's Monay started talking Baby I have a question to ask you and don't get mad! said Monay looking at Slim holding Kane and Able so she finished talking; So what you going to do now that you have two son's? asked Monay looking at Slim. But Slim just sat there holding his son's because he didn't want to say the wrong thing so he just kissed both of his son's and finished his thought's. Monay knew what that meant so she just laid back and prayed everything went well. The whole night Monay and the babies slept Slim was up thinking; and he knew he had to back out the game but he knew Freeze and Bat Man had just took that lost so he was trying to come up with a way to make sure they was good before he got out the game.

Juan was about to walk out the door until he seen Jesus and Pedro walking towards his front door, So Juan opened the door and moved to the side to let Jesus and Pedro inside. Once Jesus and Pedro took a seat Jesus gave Juan the set up. So like I was saying on the phone! We had Brother Mark and Suicide at the spot a couple of weeks ago and they gave me Slim address! said Jesus firing up a cigar. Juan was still happy that he jumped up with joy still in his eye's. So what we waiting on boss! Jesus just looked at Juan getting up to leave; You should have the address but I'll text it to you anyway!! said Jesus walking out the door headed for the car texting Juan Slim address.

Trav and Cardo was sitting in the car watching Slim old house the only time they went in the house was when they had to use the restroom or get something to eat; Slim made sure they was smoking on the best while they was on watch and they had everything they needed in the house so they was good. Five month's had almost passed since they was on watch and they was getting bored but they had order's not to kill anybody just to make the call. As day's went they was slow and the night's was slower so they spent most of there time playing chess on there phones. Until night fell and Trav had to use the phone charger in the house because Cardo was using the only one they had in the car. So Trav went to get out the car until he seen some light's coming there way so he jumped back inside and watched the car because Slim, Freeze or Bat Man would call before they just pop up.

When Juan really got the word that Slim address was in fact the right one he called Roc and Cisco with the run down because when he called them the first time he gave them order's to wait until he found out it was right. On the first ring Roc answered the phone like he hadn't been to sleep in week's. What' the deal fam! said Roc half sleep into the phone. Look you and Cisco get ready to ride with me! Remember when I called you about the information about Slim address! Well Jesus just rode over here with the same information that Havair had and everything is legit! said Juan with joy in his voice. When Roc heard that he put the phone on specker and sat up so Cisco could hear what was being said and Cisco was all ear's. And the only thing he heard was Slim address. Roc and Cisco jumped up grabbing there choppers. Where we going to meet up at! said Cisco moving towards the door. Ya'll come get me from my house! We going to handle this right away! When Roc and Cisco pulled up Juan was outside waiting on them with black bag's in both of his hands. When Juan got in he gave them the plan. Look 9 times out of 10 Slim might not be here! But his wife will be so we going to make him feel all the hurt and pain he brung on our family's! This one is for my wife!! said Juan making a cross over his heart. Roc drove down a dirt road and they seen a house with the light's off but the T.V light's was on so Roc stopped and killed the car light's Look we can't drive up there we got to just run up there and make it happen! said Roc looking at Juan in the back seat. Juan and Cisco knew that was the only way to go so everybody jumped out the S.U.V and ran towards the ranch house to the back door; when they seen it was glass Juan pulled out a hammer and broke a corner of the glass and opened the door. When the door opened Juan looked at Roc and Cisco and moved into the house with this gun's chocked and ready with Roc and Cisco on his heels. Once they split up and seen the house was empty they looked at each other and knew it was a set up so they ran out the house not known if somebody was on there way to kill them. The whole time Roc, Cisco and Juan was running towards Slim house Trav was on the phone giving him the run down from front to back after Trav gave Slim the run down they waited until the Latin King's left before they pulled off to leave.

Slim just sat in the living room of his house shacking his head. When Monay walked in she seen the twin's on the floor playing and Slim looking off in space on the sofa. So Monay walked in and stood next to Slim and started rubbing his shoulder's. What's wrong baby? asked Monay looking down at Slim. Slim just looked up at Monay with straight hurt, anger and malise in his eye's and told her what just happened. How about one of our people just called and said the Latin King's just left our old house! said Slim dropping his head in pure hurt. When Monay heard that the only thing she could do was shack her head and walk over to where the twin's was playing and laid and played with them because she knew what was about to happen to Jacksonville When Monay walked off Slim sat there for a few more minutes then he stood and walked to the game room and called Freeze and just like clock work Freeze answered talking. What the play is bruh? And how my little soulja's doing? asked Freeze smoking on a jay. But from the silence in the phone Freeze already knew it was something going on so he just played it by ear. When Freeze stopped talking Slim gave it to him raw. Bruh one of them cat's sent them Latin King's to my old house! said Slim fire hot into the phone. Freeze took the phone from his ear and looked at it and shook his head because he knew how his brother was feeling so he put the phone back to his ear and let his brother finish talking; So you already know what time it is! When you finish doing what you doing there catch the first thing smoking this way! said Slim hanging up his phone looking around thinking about how he was going to kill Brother Mark Freeze hung up the phone already known what the play was so he finished his jay thinking about how much more time Brother Mark and Suicide had on this earth.

It seemed like time was moving fast on the streets; people was getting murked every minute on the hour, Every body could feel the tension coming off of Freeze and Bat Man everything they had go on and had to do was on a time line; and they was stressing because they knew they had to find a way to knock off Pedro. Because they knew if they got him Jesus would be easy to get. So everyday Freeze and

Bat Man played the shadow's watching every move Pedro did. But every move Pedro made was a good calculated move; So they kept on watching him until he made the wrong move.

Everything was looking crazy for Juan and the Latin King's, It seemed like every since they made that bad move everything started looking sour for them in every part of the game. So Juan just sat back in his chair and tried to figure out what he was going to say when Havair or the other bosses called.

It seemed like everything was starting to look good in the hood, It was still shoot out's everyday but everything was looking good for the home front and it was looking like everybody was playing there part in this war and Freeze was getting phone calls from young nigga's ready to take flight in the street's and make a mark in the game. But Freeze and Bat Man had to much on there plate to lose focus on there number one goal and that's taking over Duval County.

Havair woke up with one thing on his mind and that was why Slim and his family was still alive, So the first thing Havair did was try and call Juan but every time he called it went to the voicemail. So Havair hung up and tried calling Juan house phone. And on the fourth ring Havair slammed his phone down and at that point Havair knew something wasn't right so he sat at his deck and even tho Havair didn't smoke weed he rolled up one of the fattest blunts on that side of the globe and sat and thanked about everything that was going on and if what he was thinking was right he needed to come up with his next move in the game.

The whole time Havair called Juan just sat looking at Havair call his cell and house phone thinking about all the heat he was feeling from everybody but while Juan sat there in his thought's he heard somebody at his front door, His first mind told him it was Havair but when he looked out the crack in the curtain he seen Miguel standing there smoking a cigarette fixing his hair in the glass. As soon as Juan opened the door Miguel mouth started running. Boy I heard all the bosses was mad with you!! said Miguel walking inside Juan house. Juan just looked and backed up so Miguel could walk in and walked to his kitchen and fixed his self a cup of coffee and sat at the breakfast bar and listened to what Migual had to say. So what happened at Slim house? asked Miguel with a slit smile on his face. Juan just looked at Miguel and picked up his coffee blew it and took a sip and sat it back down on the breakfast bar. When Miguel seen the look in Juan eye's he knew to fall back. So what's the next move? asked Miguel looking at Juan. Juan couldn't holed back how he was feeling any longer and before he knew it he had threw his cup of coffee at Miguel but Miguel moved before the coffee or the cup hit him. But Juan was in his face before he knew what happened. If you ever come into my house disrespect me I'll kill you and feed you to the gators! Miguel face had straight fear in them but he was still able to talk. Hey brother I was just playing with you! What you can't take a joke! asked Miguel fixing his jacket. Juan just looked at Miguel and turned around and walked off but before he walked out the kitchen he spoke loud enough for Miguel to hear him. And clean up that mess and get the fuck out of my house! said Juan walking down the hallway into his room and closing the door behind him.

Freeze and Bat Man was standing inside a old house watching Pedro every move. But they felt that since they been watching him for the pass 5 month's it was a waste of time so they figured they'll start watching him at his house. The first day of the watch everything was normal he had Mexican women walking around working and serving him while he sat next to the pool all day long. When night fell Bat Man pulled out the binoculars and him and Freeze watched Pedro house Bat Man was on watch so he zoomed in on Pedro window and seen him in the bed with one of the Mexican women. After Bat Man seen that he lowered his binoculars and waited until day break but they still watched his house waiting on him to slip up in any kind of way.

Inside the house Pedro woke up to the face of one of his helpers and the only thing he could do was shack his head but when he pulled the sheet's back he seen she wasn't that bad. So he woke her up and got his morning nut then sent her back to the front of the house where the other help was at. Once Pedro helper left he got up and started his day, The first thing he did was 500 push up's and sit up's and punched his punching bag for 45 minutes after he finished all that he walked in his bathroom and cleaned his self up. Once he got out the shower he could hear his phone ringing so he dried off and walked to his night stand and answered his phone. When he answered he heard Jesus so he just listened to him talk. I'm sending a car to come get you in a couple of hour's we need to have a sit down with old Brother Mark!! Ok what time is he coming? Around noon! Ok and make sure he don't have me waiting because you know how I hate to wait! said Pedro hanging up his phone walking back into the bathroom to finish getting dressed.

At the old house across the street Freeze was looking at the house and noticed it didn't have no surveillance camera's so he sat there for about 10 more minutes and a plan popped in his head. Bruh fuck just sitting in this house watching him let's make our move while all him neighbor's at work! Maybe we can catch him slipping!! Bat Man just looked until Freeze finished and grabbed his A.R 15 and moved towards the back door. When they walked to the front of the house they seen Pedro walk on the porch and look at his watch. When Freeze and Bat Man seen that there mind went to the same place and they opened fire on Pedro. When Pedro finished getting dressed he looked at his watch and seen it was 11:58 so he walk on the porch and the first place he looked was the driveway then his watch, and that was his worst mistake. The first set of bullet's ripped through Pedro body like a red hot knife ripping though butter but when Pedro fell down he hit his knee's then the second set of bullet's ripped his head clean off his shoulder's. When Freeze and Bat Man seen that they ran to there stolen car and sped off.

When the driver turned on Pedro block he seen two black guy's running towards Pedro house so he turned around and called Jesus. When Jesus got the call he was hurt because his first mind told him to ride over there but he wanted to chill with the two beautiful Colombian women he had instead of going and handling the business at hand. So now that left him with no back up so Jesus jumped up and ran to his closet and grabbed a Russian military issued chopper, and sat to his table loading up his drum because he knew they was after him next and he wanted to be ready when they came.

Thing's was looking good for Freeze and Bat Man; They had the streets where they wanted them at so Freeze and Bat Man sat at the trap playing chess when lil Boss called Freeze with some info. That was

Lil Boss talking about people riding around putting up flyers talking about Suicide big birthday bash! And he gave me the address where they having it at, But I think it might be a set up or something! said Freeze passing Bat Man his phone to show him the address. Bat Man just looked at the address and something just hit him and told him that something wasn't right that Freeze was telling him. Bruh on some real nigga shit we both know we ain't going to be there! He just trying to through us off so we need to make our move fast! said Bat Man handing Freeze back his phone. Freeze grabbed his phone and was looking because he knew everything Bat Man said was the truth.

Havair was on the phone trying to get in contact with Juan but everybody he called said the same thing. Either they haven't seen him or they haven't talked to him so Havair sat back down madder than he was the day before.

Juan sat in the house trying to come up with the best move but every move he made was a dead end so he just laid back and waited for anything to fall through for him.

Since the sit down with the Latin King's Suicide knew he had to make calculated moves, He wasn't worried about the Latin King's; He was more worried about Freeze, Slim and Bat Man so he sat in his office and made all his phone calls he needed to make once he finished making his calls he sat back thinking and what he was about to do, and he knew what he was about to do was some fuck nigga shit but he knew that was the only was he was going to win even if he was in the ground. So Suicide stood up and knocked over both kings on the chess board. Freeze watched Suicide every move while Bat Man watched Jesus every move. But Bat Man got all his info he needed to make his move so he sat back and watched and waited for the right move.

Jesus was still in his house scared to move when he got a phone call from his pastor, When he seen the number he started not to answer but something on the inside told him to mash talk when he did he heard his pastor voice. Hello my son!! I haven't seen you in a month or so is everything alright I've been worried so I figured I'll call and check on you and see how everything was going with you! said the pastor worried about his sheep. Juan just sat there and listened to his pastor until he finished then he spoke. Well father everything been going ok I'll be there this Sunday! That's good my son I'll see you then! said the pastor hanging up the phone praying that his sheep would really wake up and leave the game alone. Jesus hung up his phone and laid down on the sofa he had in front of the door... But Jesus didn't know the danger he had in front of his house.

Bat Man was in Jesus across the street neighbor shed watching all movements that went on in Jesus house and yard then Bat Man seen a limo turn on Jesus street so Bat Man ran to his splack and waited on the corner for Jesus to leave his house Sunday morning came so fast that Jesus was having second thoughts about going. But when his driver showed up he had know choice but to go. Jesus got up moving slow but when he went in the kitchen and made a fresh pot of coffee he started moving a little bit faster. It took him a whole hour to eat and get dressed for Sunday service. When Jesus walked outside the first thing he did was look both ways then he walked to the limo with his chopper off safety. The whole time Jesus got in the limo he never seen the car following behind them.

The whole ride Bat Man never knew where they was going until the limo pulled inside a church parking lot so Bat Man parked across the street and waited until he seen people walking back outside the church.

Jesus walked inside the church greeting people shacking hands in a good mode so Jesus sat on the front row and listened to the good word that the pastor was saying until the service was over and people started to walk out so Jesus stayed back so he could talk to the pastor on a one on one. After the pastor shook everybody hand and made sure the church was clear he walked over to where Jesus was sitting and touched his knee. What's the problem my child! A tear rolled down Jesus face when the pastor asked him that question so he whipped his eye's and gave the pastor the uncut story. Pastor I've been marked for death! And I don't know when it's coming it could be today or next week and I don't know what to do right now! said Jesus with his head down and tears flown down his face. The pastor just sat there and listened and felt all the pain in his words but he had know answers for him so he did the only thing he knew any man would do and that was pray for his soul.

Bat Man sat outside the whole service and waited until he seen the doors open and people walking outside but he didn't see Jesus then he seen Jesus limo drive around the back of the church so Bat Man jumped out of his splack and ran to the drive side window of the limo and shot the driver in the head with the silenced 40 Cal he had, Then he posted up behind the door and waited on Jesus to walk out.

After the prayer Jesus finished talking to his pastor then he texted his driver to pull up around the back of the church by the back door. After Jesus got the text from his driver telling him he was there Jesus started walking towards the door after he gave his pastor his tie's.

When Jesus walked out the sun almost blind him so he stopped and covered his eye's and when he moved his hand what he seen almost killed him Bat Man stood behind the door for almost 45 minutes before the back door flew open and Jesus walked out and covered his eye's. That's when Bat Man lifted his 40 and when Jesus moved his hand the first bullet Bat Man shot hit Jesus in his throat but Jesus was still moving so he walked over him and shot him 4 more times in the face and ran back to his splack and drove to the safe house to meet up with Freeze to go over there power move on Suicide.

Freeze was on post watching Suicide every move from the time he woke up until the time he went to sleep it was going on 3 weeks before anything happened. Freeze was following behind Suicide when he seen Suicide pull into a bar parking lot on the west side. So Freeze waited across the street in a business parking lot and waited on Suicide to walk out. After about 6 hours of waiting Freeze seen Suicide walking out but who Freeze seen him walking with threw him for a loop he wasn't expecting to see him walk out with Brother Mark. After they parted ways Freeze was in motion about to follow Suicide Bat Man called him to meet up at the safe house so Freeze turned off thinking about why Brother Mark would call Suicide to meet up with him at a bar of all places.

Suicide was running late with his meeting with his ace in the whole. When Suicide pulled up into the parking garage he seen a all black S.U.V and pulled up besides it grabbed a envelope hopped in the passenger seat and closed the door When Suicide got in the driver was on the phone but as soon as he finished he looked straight at Suicide When the chief of police ended his phone call Suicide gave him the lay out Like I was telling you the last time we talked!

I feel like my two nephews is out to kill me! And I don't know when they coming! said Suicide holding his head down while he snitched on Freeze and Slim. The chief just sat there and looked confused when Suicide said that, because he remembered the first time he met Freeze they saved his life so that made chief Sappe sit and think.

When Suicide seen the look on his friend face he knew he had to get to the point. So he just gave his friend the whole run down. Ok Brother Mark gave the Latin King's Slim and Freeze address and they went through there to kill him but they had already moved! So we know they know it was us so I'm just trying to get a back up plan so I need you to start a small investigation on there to give me and Mark enough time to get out of the country! said Suicide with straight fear in his eye's. Chief Sappe felt bad but he knew he had to do it so he grabbed the envelope and looked at the money and put it in his arm rest Suicide opened his car door and slide in his car and pulled off thinking about the snitch shit he just done but he knew that was the only move he had in the game.

When Freeze pulled up he seen Bat Man car parked on the side of the house so Freeze parked beside Bat Man and walked inside the house straight to the game room and seen Bat Man sitting at the chess board smoking a jay looking deep into the game. But when he seen Freeze walking through the door he bust out laughing because he knew it was about to be some crazy shit. Bruh guess where I ran into old boy at? Freeze just looked because they done murked nigga's everywhere so he knew it had to be in a crazy place. Where he was at? asked Freeze looking confused. He was leaving the church house! And I hit his bitch ass when he was walking out that mother fucker! said Bat Man laughing. Freeze just looked at Bat Man and shook his head. Nigga you the Mother Fucking Devil!! said Freeze laughing hard at Bat Man. Bat Man just looked then started laughing because he already knew that was going to be the first thing said. After Bat Man finished laughing Freeze told him what he just seen... Nigga how bout I just seen Suicide and brother Mark meeting up at a bar on the West side!! Batman straighten up real fast when he heard that his focus was on everything Freeze had to say from that point on. So you know I been watching this nigga!! So I found out that he suppose to be at this little bash on his birthday!! So we need to make that move when his guard down and that's on his birthday!! Batman was in his zone because Suicide bash was in three weeks and he knew that Freeze was going to make a statement. The only thing Batman could say was one thing. I'm ready when you is bruh!!

When Haviar heard about Jesus he was on fire the only thing was on his mind was finding a way to talk to Juan, because he needed answers now and the only person he knew would pass that message for him was Roc, so the first thing he did was call Roc cell phone, on the first ring he heard Roc voice. Haviar didn't give him a chance to say nothing.

"Look" tell your brother he better be to the room in a month from today!! "that's 30 days" to have Slim, Freeze and Batman dead!! and I'm going to be looking at the news everyday just to make sure he handled his business!! before Roc could say anything Haviar had hung up his phone. Roc had the phone on speaker so cisco heard everything that Haviar said and they knew that things was looking real crazy with all five of the head field Latin Kings dead and nothing happening to Slim, Freeze or Batman they was getting pressure from everywhere, from different states and all was calling and they only wanted to know is they dead yet, and how it happened, but nobody had the answers they wanted to hear so they gave them all a deadline to have Slim, Freeze and Batman dead, and the way everything was looking they was going to miss that deadline. It seem like everything they do they be one step ahead of them, so they was just trying to find out anything that could get them anywhere closer to them but everybody they got or grabbed didn't know nothing about no houses or traps or anything. So they was just really killing for nothing so everything was just fucked up, so Roc & Cisco got up and drove to Juan house.

It was midnight when they pulled up to Juan house, from the outside looking in it looked like nobody was home, but Roc knew he was home, and he had the spare key ever since the incident happened, when they walked in, the house looked like nobody was there until they walked in the pool house and seen him laying on a sofa bed watching TV.

When he seen Roc and Cisco he knew it was Haviar because he been getting the same phone calls everybody else been getting.

So he turned the TV off and turned around to face them. "What do ya'll need?" I don't give a fuck what type of time you on but you need to get the fuck up and do something because you really got us looking bad right now!!

The whole time Roc talked Cisco just stood there shaking his head because the way Juan was looking it looked like he had done gave up on himself and everything he stood for... "so you need to get your soft ass up and do something because this shit is looking real shitty for us so get off your fuck ass and make a move or call a move!! "and" Haviar gave us 30 days to have Slim, Freeze and Batman dead!!

Juan just dropped his head because now he had to worry about his one family if he did have this hit done on the deadline. So Juan stood up and walked over to the bar and fixed himself a drink and thought of a good way to hit them but every thought he came up with was like a death trap, so he down that drink and poured another and sat at the bar and put his mind to the test, then he remembered that Jesus said they had a meeting with Suicide and brother Mark, so Juan knew they had to go see brother Mark, but he had to find out where brother Mark was.

Brother Mark was at his first house this was a house he first got when he first entered the game, slim was the only person who knew where this house was but it's been 20 years since they left and he knew Slim didn't know that he still keep it in living condition so he just layed low because he heard about the five Kings that Slim, Freeze and Batman killed, and about the Kings bad hit on Slim old house. Brother Mark knew his day was numbered so he just sat around the house reading the word trying to get back right with the Heavenly Father because he knew that he had the kings and Slim looking for him and in his eyes he'll rather let Slim take him out, but in brother Mark eye's he wasn't going to let nobody kill him.

Slim twin boys "Kane and Able" was getting big he spent so much time with them that it kind of got his mind off the problem with brother

Mark but Monay keep asking him when was brother Mark going to be dismissed.

So one night after Slim and Monay put Kane and Able to sleep they walked to their bedroom, Slim laid in the bed why Monay went in the bathroom and freshened up while Slim rolled up a blunt for him and a paper jay for Monay. When Monay came out the bathroom she walked out with just a thong on and walked over to the bed and seen her jay and put fire to it.

After they finished smoking they laid back and watched Friday. When the movie went off Monay went back to on Demand and was looking for another movie to watch, when Slim sensed something wrong with Monay and asked her what was on her mind, and she said what Slim wasn't trying to hear.

I don't feel safe knowing Mark is still alive, and me and the boys have family in Duval and I want to see my mother and she wants to see her grandsons and hold them!! Not look at them on a picture!! Slim just looked because he knew that everything in Duval was almost over but he couldn't keep her out of Duval for too much longer but he knew it wasn't safe for her and the kids to be in Duval now. So Slim told her the best thing he could come up with. "Bae" one minute you tell me you want me out the game now you telling me you want to visit your mother in Duval!! and you already know how that shit looking in Duval!! Why would you put me in this type of spot? Then with Mark, he'll be gone when I hit Duval.

Freeze and Batman already murked the Kings, he gave us the addresses to so everything looking good for us bae! Please just chill and let me handle what I need to handle on my end, please!!

Monay just laid back in Slim arms and kissed him on the jaw and she fell asleep about 20 minutes later. So Slim just sat back and thought about the way everything was going and things was looking very good for him and their team. He talked to Freeze and Batman and everything should be done in a few weeks.

So he knew he had to have everything in order for when that day come he'll be ready to move, so Slim slide out the bed and walked in the room with his boys and prayed they didn't grow up like him, Freeze

Freezing in Duval

and Batman, after he kissed them on their forehead he walked in the game room and turned on ESPN and laid on the sofa and fell asleep.

The time had come for every big name from Duval to come out bigga rankin was hosting the bash you had everybody coming from Boosie to T.I but the opening show was the Urko Ballers.

Everybody was vibing to the music it was over 4,000 people showed up it was free food and drinks, everybody was still pulling into Lonnie Miller Park but the police came and shut the party down but the real show was going to be a the "Bottom Up's Gentleman's Club" Suicide was already at the club. Chilling, him and his few partners he had, he had paid for the club for the whole night so he sat around watching all the half naked females dancing on the stage and giving all his old school partners lap dance, until the head of security walked over to Suicide and bent down an asked him was he ready to let the people in and Suicide gave him the thumbs up and the security guard walked to the door and people started to come in like a water fall.

Freeze and Batman had everything set up, they had got word form one of the dancers that Suicide and a few of his partners was having the after party at "Bottom-Up" and the security guard had a list of names so Freeze knew it was a very small list, so Freeze spent all week trying find the right inside person until Batman reminded him that the owner of the club did business with them, so Freeze called and made everything happen for him.

He had paid the owner 30,000 to leave the back door open for them so once they had that covered they waited until the owner called him and told him Suicide had showed up and he had the club paid for until 5 AM.

Once Freeze got the call they loaded up and got into a stolen car they had for almost 6 months, the whole ride Freeze mind was on how he was going to kill him. Was it going to be fast or slow.

Suicide was in Bottoms Up feeling himself he had the owner bring him a trash bag with 50, 000 dollars in one dollar bills, Suicide grabbed the bag and walked to the stage and started throwing fist full of money to the females on the stage. Then he grabbed the bag and dumped it on the stage and called for the owner to bring him another bag of 50,000, after 2 hours of thrown money at the dancers and 250,000 Suicide grabbed two of the females and walked them to the V.I.P.

Freeze and Batman was on the South side at the Bottom's Up Gentleman's Club but traffic was so bad that they had to park two blocks away in a plaza and walked to the club. They had to wait until the people moved from by the door before they made their move.

It was about 30 minutes before the people moved from view of the door, so Freeze and Batman walked to the door and checked it and it was open, so they walked in... when Freeze and Batman walked in they seen the few people that was on the guess list walking around. Some was tipping and some was betting on the pool table, they just sat and watched everybody's movements in the club because they had to find out where Suicide was and fast so they sat back and watched everything until they seen some people going into the V.I.P. Freeze knew that was going to be hard to do, so he watched the V.I.P. And had Batman watching everybody else in the club.

In the V.I.P. Suicide had his shirt open with his pants down getting some slow neck on the old skool sofa they had back there, with about four more of his partners was back there to handle their business.

When all the other people walked form out the back the security made one of their worst mistakes. When they unlocked the door and started letting people out the club. When Freeze and Batman seen everybody focus on leaving they walked in the V.I.P. Freeze walked to Suicide while Batman made sure everybody else stayed where they was and didn't move. When Suicide seen Freeze he knew his ticket was pushed, and the only thing he could do was drop his head in hurt and shame because he knew that everything was his fault.

The only thing Freeze could do was look at him and smile. After Freeze smiled he left Suicide with a message. Most niggaz would ask you why and all that other fuck shit!! but I'm just about to tell you two things!! "one is" I'm going to send the rest of your team where you going!! and two is check-mate!! Then Freeze raised his silenced 40 cal and unloaded every bullet in Suicide body and reloaded another clip and unloaded that one inside his body, before he changed clips again and him and Batman left out with no problems.

Freezing in Duval

The streets was so hot after the murder of Suicide that every side had to sit back and just play the streets by ear. Juan was looking crazy now because he knew shit was real on the field now and they need to do something and something fast, but the streets was so hot to the only thing he could do was chill.

Shit was so hot until Freeze had to plan a road trip so after he made sure everything was good he loaded up his S.U.V. And hit "I95 North"

The whole ride Freeze was thinking about everything that had happened in the last 18 months from Baby-Face and their unborn seed to Suicide working with the Latin Kings, and brother Mark sending the Kings to kill Slim.

Shit was crazy. The death toll in Duval was over the chart's people was scared to come out their house because of all the killing that was going around town. So Batman just moved around still killing all the Kings workers and doing all the homework on the other head Kings.

Slim, Monay and the boys Kane and Able was waiting on Freeze to come and give them the run down on everything that went down in da ville since he been gone.

Monay was cooking and slim was rolling up blunts waiting on Freeze to pull up, because he couldn't figure out why it was so hot. But he knew that was how Duval was and they knew how to get around all of that, so he sat at the chess board and just sat there looking at the board until Kane and Able walked in and he grabbed Kane and Able sat across from his father and Slim just looked at Able playing with the chess pieces and he knew right then he was going to be the problem. Freeze hit North Carolina and had to put Slim address in his GPS to find it because he was ducked off good in the country, it took Freeze about two hours for the GPS to pick up on Slim house. When Freeze pulled up to Slim house all the lights was on so he grabbed his bags and walked in. As soon as Kane and Able seen Freeze they ran and jumped in his arms. When Slim and Monay heard Kane and Able screaming in joy Slim walked to the game room and sat at the chess board on the white side and moved the white pawn.

Monay walked in the kitchen and finished cooking, when Freeze finished with the boys he walked in the kitchen and kissed Monay on the chick and walked out headed to the game room to holla at Slim. When Freeze walked in the hallway he didn't know how Slim was going to take to what he was about to say, but Freeze walked in and seen Slim at the chess board on the white side with a pawn moved. "Nigga" sit down!! let's push one!! Freeze already knew he had to push one because they haven't pushed one in a long time. So Freeze walked up and dapped Slim and they sat and ran the best out of five.

When they finished they was two-two and stale-mate.

After they set the pieces back up, Slim grabbed two rolled up blunts and passed Freeze one and got the run down live from the horse's mouth. After Freeze finished telling Slim what the play was, both to them was thrown off so they blazed up two more jay and sat back trying to come up with something because Slim felt like he moved somewhere else because everything was about to end and the twins was about to start Head-Start so he had to make his next move his best move.

Freeze sat thinking because he knew something big was going to happen but he knew he had to thing outside the box from this point on, and he knew Slim was going to probably move just because the boys was about to start school soon or Head-Start whatever they call it, Freeze just stayed in his zone, and Slim was in his zone.

It was Monday morning at J.S.O. Headquarters, the chief of Police Sappe called a mandatory meeting for all the head of Narcotics and Violent crimes units for that afternoon.

When he got the news about how they caught him with his pants down at that strip club he knew he had to put something together fast because he already knew how Freeze thing when he got his mind set, so he knew he had to stop him and fast.

When Chief Sappe walked in the room all the Head's was there, after he greeted everybody he stood in front of a board and showed pictures. Then he started to talk about all the killings and drugs was behind them and their war with the Latin Kings.

So after Chief Sappe finished with the projector the only words came out his mouth was... Who want to work the Slim and Freeze case because their names been ringing all around town so I need ya'll to find out what's the word on them or find something on them.

Freezing in Duval

Everybody was looking around trying to figure out who the Chief was talking to until Det. T. Smith and B. Jennings stood up. Now I want the rest of ya'll to find some Bank statements overseas and in the states. That's how the meeting ended, everybody went to go do their job. As Det. T. Smith and B. Jennings left the police station, Det. Smith sat in the driver's seat at the red light when he came up with the perfect plan; hey bruh on some real nigga shit you know what time it is with me!!! "Hell mother fucking yeah" We get money fuck working!! "well" this what I came up with. I grew up with Slim went to school together, so when we go holla at him everything should be good, that sound good bruh! But when we going to see him? We'll go Monday afternoon while we making rounds! That's what's up I could use that spare change.

At the Sunset Inn Juan walked inside the sweet and seen his boss face was on murder mode and wasn't a good sight.

"Haviar" why in the fuck that cock sucking nigga ain't burping dirt yet? I haven't found out where his new spot is at boss but when... fuck that shit you talking about I want him and his fuck ass cock sucking friend dead right along side Slim!! I want this done in a week no later than 8 days starting today so get the fuck out of my room and do your fucking job before you make me do my job!! The only thing Juan could do was walk out the door and hit the stair case.

At Slim house, Slim and Freeze was coming up with a plan to leave Slim old house when Freeze cell-phone ringed! "Hello" who dis!! Nigga this Rosco!! some police came round here looking for Slim he said he knew him from school or something! "What his name is? Did he leave a card? or something!! "Yeah he left a card!! and said it's for your own good that we call him ASAP!! "What his name is, bruh? It's! Hold on!! Here it go! It say Det. T. Smith!!" That's what's up bruh!! "Ok" good tell the rest of the crew that we on our way home! And everybody need to be at the spot!! It's a mandatory meeting!! "Nigga asap"!! I got ya bruh 10-4" Freeze hung up the phone and sat down not knowing how he was going to break this bad news to Slim. "Hey Slim" that was Rosco! He said some fuck ass police man came by looking for you and said he need to see you asap! It's for your own good if you do... "what he said the cracker name is?" I think he said his name was T. Smith, yeah that's it!! "T. Smith" I know that soft ass cracker!! We went to school together! I heard he was a cop!! but now his ass fucked up!! because as fuck up as we is in the game! So if he on the same page we on!! then we could put him on our payroll!! "All that sound real good bruh!! but can we trust him at all? Or what you think cause we can use him but can we trust him? "I feel where you coming from on that! "but" if we can't we can always kill him and his partner!!" Well that mean we're on the same page!! But we need to hurry up, our plane leave at 3:00!! So come on you know you move real slow!! "Nigga" come on I been ready! "Let's go".

Batman was at his hide out sitting and thinking about everything that was happening and going on when his house phone rung... "Who this is? Nigga it's me!! your boy!! "Nigga" I feel good, I think it's bout to go down!! You ready to murk some shit? "Hell fuck yeah" I been sitting in this stank ass house to dam long! I been ready bruh! "What the play is? Slim and Freeze on their way here now!! and they called a mandatory meeting and you know when we have those somebody crossed that line!!

It might be that nigga Slim was cool with that crossed him, if that's it I'm going to off him real soon!! "But bruh" before you do anything let me know first!! so I can be right there! I never liked that fuck niggga anyway!!

I always seen the fuck nigga in him but "bruh" I was just letting you know what the play was! I got you bruh! If Slim or Freeze put me on that job I'll hit you up!! but call me as soon as there plane land so I'll be there at the spot when they get there!! "I got ya bruh".

On the plane ride to Jacksonville, Slim and Freeze sat in first class thinking about what's been going on. When Slim started talking... "Bruh" the first thing I'm going to do is find that fuck nigga Mark and kill his fuck ass G-shit bruh!! "We going to let Batman handle that!! But what we going to do for product? "Bruh" I feel where you coming from with that but with the cash we got!! we can buy anything we want!! But first we need to handle this problem before it handle us!! "Bruh you dead ass right" but I think them police boys can handle this for us, because my gut tell me them crackers need the money! That's what I mean!! We pay them 30 thousand a month and they'll let us run the streets how we want! And they'll kill on demand!! "Shit bruh" I hope so!! It sound sweet!! We'll just sit back and see how everything play out.

On the Riverside on Oak street two Russian women, walked inside a bar, when they walked in all eyes was looking their way, they was the finest bitches that walked in, so everybody just looked until they walked towards the back of the bar. When one of the ladies walked to this ugly looking guy but nobody had the heart to laugh at him or make a joke. "Zoya" "Hey boss" you wanted us here tonight that let me know you have a job for us to do, is that right? Gosha just sat there waiting on all the eyes to get off the girls before he talked... "We're having a meeting in the back we'll talk then we need ya'll ladies!! Gosha got up and the ladies followed behind him until they entered a room filled with Russian Mafia bosses.

When they walked in, the room got real still. So Gosha broke all the silence in the room. Now that everybody's here the meeting can start!! Well! Let's get to know each other!! These are the killers I was telling you guys about!

Lev, one of the Mafia bosses bust into a load of laugh when Gosha said that... Man I done heard some funny shit!! but these is two little fucking girls I can't put my trust and money on these two bitches "Well Lev" I can only tell ya'll what I know about them!!

Every job they ever did was the best! Clean and never miss the mark, always hit!! and I'll put my life on these two women here!! Yura just looked from one face to another then stood so the room could see him!!

So you say these the best of the best!! and you put your soul on it!! So on that note the meeting can begin!! Gosha stood and the meeting started.

As we all know our business is expanding all over Jacksonville!! We're going to start on the East Side then move our business to the West Side!! Right now everybody popping pills and they buying them from us. The only thing we have to do is have better product than everybody!! then we'll see all the money!! Yura couldn't take much more before he had to get his thought off his chest. "Now everything sound good but What about the other dealers? That's where the girls come in at!!

When the dealers don't want to buy our product!! then we send these sexy ladies in!! and the rest is history!! As the meeting was wrapping up the door man passed out the bosses' coats and hats and the bosses left out the back. The ladies walked out the front of the bar and drove off.

At the Omni Hotel Slim and Freeze sat in their sweet getting ready for the meeting. Slim was making sure every dot was in line, "bruh make sure Rosco bring that card! That cracker left him! I'm on point with that bruh!! I already texted everybody! And I told him to bring that card with him! So that's handled!! The only thing we have to do is wait! So while we wait let's have a drink. As Freeze and Slim poured their drink they heard a hard knock on the door, but Freeze already knew who it belonged to... when Freeze opened the door Batman, Rosco, Cardo, Baldy and Lil Boss walked inside the room all smiles.

Slim, what it do fam!! It's been a long time coming!! Everybody greeted Slim and Freeze with pounds and hugs "but Rosco" here's this card bruh!! that a crazy ass cracker!! He just jumped out his car talking and vibing like we and him grow up together or something!! but from what I see the cracker kool! "Hell yeah" that's what we need an inside man!! That'll let us know if we too hot and help us move fast if we too cold!! but that let me know that the team is stronger now!! we making all the right moves!! but we need to handle every loose end we got!! Cardo just sat listening to everything everybody had to say before he spoke his peace!! I understand everything!! but we need to handle them "Kings" first and for most!! "Well before me and Freeze start this meeting I want everybody drinking or have a drink close by. While everybody fixed their drinks Slim started... "First thing first" we got a lot of shit going on and it's time for everybody to put in work!! Everybody who say their Jack-Boys it's time to start jacking!! No man will sit around and chill!! We got a whole city we beating and killing!! and we bout to take over!!

So this is how we going to play this!! first I want Lil. Boss, Baldy and Trav, it's time to put your money where you're at I know ya'll got heart!! but I want to see ya'll under pressure!! so I came up with the best way to find that out is to form a team and I want Baldy with Rosco!! Lil. Boss with Batman!! and Trav you with Cardo!!

Freezing in Duval

Now the reason for these teams is that I want these Kings dead real soon!! The faster they die!! the faster ya'll can take this shit over "Freeze" What the fuck you mean bruh? You said "ya'll" like your not a part of the team no more!! "well like I said!! I've been in this game for so long and it's time for me to move on I've made my share of money in this game so I feel ya'll is ready for this shit!!

I'm just making sure ya'll have enough bread to last ya'll and ya'll family!! "Bruh fuck that!! this your boy Freeze!! We in it to win it!! Bruh if you out I'm out!! Freeze sat there looking for a response. When Batman jumped up!! "man ya'll mean to tell me ya'll gone out the game "Ok, ok" this how this will work!! I love ya'll niggaz the same way!! So this how I'm playing this!! I'll still be in the game!! but it'll be in the back ground!! I'll put all the money up on the first run!! When ya'll finish I get my cash off top then ya'll keep it going!!

We'll see how everything play out!! but that's the law!!

Rosco couldn't hold his joy and jumped off his bar stool. "Hell yeah bruh!! That's what I'm talking about!! Nigga on a come up!! I wish a nigga would!! "Hold on bruh" me and Freeze was thinking bout the next move!! and we came up with the X-pills!! everybody doing them!! but the number one goal is to stay on point at all time!! No matter what!! when ya'll make a move everybody come back!! any questions? As Slim looked around Cardo started to talk. Hell yeah bruh you right!! but really the new shit is "molly" everybody doing them and it's more money and cheaper!!

This nigga I know that's eating on the beach say it sales just like coke but it have the feelingof 10 X-pills, Freeze bruh!! I told him bout molly's these bitches go in on them mollys that's that play on my end!! I'm bout that call cardo!! I feel ya'll! After all this!! I'l check on that!! but before we go and finish our night!! It's one more thing!! It's a problem that's been on my mind and it's time for him to go; many of ya'll knew him and some will never meet him!!

Batman knew this was his time to finally kill Mark, bruh you must be talking about that fuck nigga Mark!! "Hell yeah" that nigga must die for crossing me and that go for anyone of you little niggaz here tonight!!

This is something I want ya'll to live by-die by!! Nothing beat the cross but the double cross so that's some real nigga shit for ya. So take it how you want to take it!! The right way and live a long time rich!! but take it the fucked-up way and die real fast and real ugly!! By Batman being the loose cannon he had to put icing on the cake.

So it's on record!! the first one of ya'll fuck up the last thing you see is me!! So it's time to do what you get paid to do!!

At the Sunset in Juan was sitting replaying everything in his mind from the first time he ever laid eyes on Slim, he knew from that day he was going to be a major problem one day. Now that problem got his family looking at him with fire in their eyes.

Juan was knocked out of his daze when he heard his phone ring... Shit! Fuck!! Fuck!! "Hello" what's up Boss, how... "Fuck the hello's" I've been looking at the news and I haven't seen anyone of those niggaz yet? I'm sitting thinking about that now!! It's going to take some time for... you dumb mother fucker!!

How dare you raise your voice up at me!! if you don't have these niggaz killed in two days!! "Haviar, please!! Sir I'll have this handled!! just please give me a little more time so I could put everything together!! Look this is not a fuck toy you playing with!! We been going at it with him for too long!! It's time for him and his crew to leave this world!! So you got three days to kill these niggaz!! If you don't you already know I'm coming and when I come I'm coming alone!! "Yes Sir"

At the meeting with Smith and Jennings, Slim and Freeze sat facing them while Slim talked. Well first!! I want to say good afternoon!! Now let's get to the matter at hand!! "ok" ya'll know what me and my brother do! And the business we in!! we need you and your friend to guaranty we stay good in the game!! and we'll make sure ya'll have a early retirement!!

Since Slim only looked at Smith, Smith did all the talking!! That's why we came to talk to ya'll!! because we felt ya'll could use our help out here!! We can help with our people! And we can clean anybody out here on the streets for you!! That's why we talking!! Now because I have a lot of shit going on in these streets!!

So every helping hand I get will do me some good! Well we'll start ya'll off with 30 thousand a month and 10 thousand every head!! How that sound? That sound real sweet bruh!! We'll do what we need to do on our end of the deal!! and you make sure cash on deck on time!! Well today is the 15th!! Here's the first month pay here!! and any other payments come when I call!! I give the name!! you clean!! Same rules go for ya'll two!! If you cross me you die!!

I promise that like I promise ya'll money on point every month!!

Do we have a deal? I have no problem at all bruh!!!

At the trap house everybody was there talking about their next move. Batman was off the deep end every since Slim gave him word, "fuck this shit we need to kill these fuck ass Kings tonight!! the faster the better!! I'm with that there!! "bruh shit" we can ride now!! I don't give a flying fuck bruh!! Shit cardo I'm riding too!!

I'm sick of just talking!! It's time for my fire to do all my talking for me!! "Jitt" you ain't going to do a mother fucking thing but fuck up!! and if we slip they grip!! Hey Rosco, nigga you got me all the way fucked up!! "Nigga" I ain't never been a jitt in my life!!

Since I been 12 I've been robbing Peter to pay Paul!! So don't ever try me like that!! and nigga I don't fuck-up!!

Alright little nigga we going to see about all that mouth you got little nigga!! Man back to what I was saying before all you niggaz started running your mouth!! Some of them Kings be at the Sunset Inn by the West-Gate!! The way it's set-up!! We'll have to wait, but the whole sweet thing is that I got a little bitch that work for house cleaning I'll get her to get me a key to their room and the rest is history!! but Batman I was brought up never to trust a bitch! And you know what!! "Your dead right" that's why she have to die with them...

www.ingramcontent.com/pod-product-compliance
Lightning Source LLC
LaVergne TN
LVHW041608070526
838199LV00052B/3035